To my mother
and to the memory of my father

Brenda Schenkel

A CAREER ROMANCE FOR YOUNG MODERNS

LORNA EVANS
SOCIAL WORKER

Books by Rega Kramer McCarty

BRENDA BECOMES A BUYER

LORNA EVANS: SOCIAL WORKER

LORNA EVANS
SOCIAL WORKER

by REGA KRAMER McCARTY

JULIAN MESSNER, INC. • NEW YORK

Published by Julian Messner, Inc.
8 West 40 Street, New York 18

Published simultaneously in Canada
by The Copp Clark Publishing Co. Limited

© Copyright 1961 by Rega Kramer McCarty

Printed in the United States of America

Library of Congress Catalog Card No. 61-13826

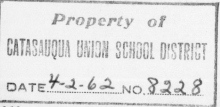

*I would like to express my thanks to the following Tacoma social workers for
their help:*

Miss Eunice Allen, Director, Tacoma Community House
Miss Catherine Anzivino, Director, Family Service Agency
Mr. Bruce Brady, Administrative Director, United Good Neighbor Organization
Miss Laura De Veuve, Executive Director, YWCA
Miss Kathleen Hall, Family Service Agency Counselor
Mr. Theodore Marchesini, Family Court Commissioner
Mrs. Erna Parker, Director, School Program for Elementary Schools
Mr. George Parrott, Social Worker, Western State Hospital
Lt. Carl Peterson, Youth Guidance, Police Department
Mr. Howard Rosen, Child Guidance Clinic
Mr. Rudolph Voth, Social Worker, Western State Hospital
Miss Joan Weber, Director of Group Work Department, YWCA
Mrs. Essie Wolfrom, Children's Welfare Division, Department of Public As-
sistance

Chapter One

Lorna Evans noted with dismay that the hands of the desk clock pointed to ten minutes past six. There remained a case report to write, the Y.W.C.A. bulletin to complete . . . and she had promised Farley that she would be ready for the party at eight. Even now she would have to hurry—Farley was always prompt—and this was one date for which she had wanted to take special pains with her appearance. Farley's friends had planned this party in honor of Milli Mercer, who had just returned from abroad.

According to all reports Milli was strictly *femme-fatale* material, and promised to be quite a threat where Farley was concerned. In fact, she had been engaged to him before going to Europe. Lorna wondered what had happened to that romance. But, she told herself, there was no point worrying about it—Farley wouldn't have invited her to the party if he had preferred Milli, would he? . . . Yet she had to admit that she *was* worried. Having known him only four months, could she compete with a girl who had dated him since their high school days?

Lorna had come straight from the Graduate School of Social Work at the University of Washington to Tacoma to take a job as Assistant Secretary at the Young Women's Christian Association. Her family was far from wealthy, and she had studied very hard in college so that she could make a career for herself and pay her parents back. Lorna was serious about her work and had not expected to be caught up in a gay social whirl in Tacoma—but she had not counted on meeting Farley Knowles, either. Now she often found herself torn between the many extra responsibilities at the Y, which she wanted to take on, and the party, movie, and dinner dates, which she enjoyed too much to refuse.

Closing her typewriter, Lorna sighed and gave a last glance at the clock. She'd have to get to work earlier than usual tomorrow if she hoped to catch up on all the little details that made her job such a busy and essential one. She hurried into her tweed coat and turned out the light in her office, noting that darkness fell earlier now that the Northwest's rainy season was approaching. She was on the landing when she heard voices in the lobby below. One sounded like a young girl's and it carried an undertone of urgency:

"Isn't there *anyone* here I could talk to? A counselor or something?"

The other voice belonged to Mrs. Whitney, the desk clerk. "I'm sorry but the staff has gone for the day. There'll be someone here later, if you care to wait."

"Well, no . . . I guess not."

The uncertainty, the distress, in the young voice immediately stirred Lorna's sympathy. She moved into the shadow of the stairway landing recess so that she could see the speakers without being seen herself. Standing at the desk was a fragile-looking girl, wearing a coat too large for her and clutching a shabby purse and overnight bag. "I should speak to her," Lorna told herself, "she seems to be in trouble. But if I do, I'll have no time to spare when I get home." She knew that Bea Miller, who was in charge of the teen-age program, would arrive around seven and could talk to her.

"Is there something I could do for you?" Mrs. Whitney was asking.

"I—I don't think so . . . I'm sorry I bothered you. I guess I'd better be going." The girl gave the desk clerk a trembling smile and turned toward the front door.

What if this child *is* in trouble and I let her go! Lorna hesitated no longer and ran down the remaining steps. "Just a moment," she called after the retreating figure. "I'm Lorna Evans, one of the staff. May I help you?"

As the girl paused and then slowly started to walk back to the desk, Lorna had a few seconds to view her more closely. Her dark hair was cut in a pixie style, emphasizing the gamin-like quality of her face; but her solemn brown eyes did not have the mischievous twinkle that one might have expected to find in them. She seemed somewhat on the defensive, but at the same time there was an appealing, half-apologetic air about her.

"Oh Miss Evans! I thought you had left. This young lady wanted to speak to someone . . ." Mrs. Whitney was explaining.

"Are you a counselor?" the girl asked shyly.

"I suppose you could call me that. In any case, if you have a problem perhaps I can help you."

"Well, perhaps you can." The girl regarded Lorna gravely. "Could you spare a few minutes? You were on your way out just now . . ."

Since she still seemed uncertain, Lorna realized that she'd have to decide the issue if she was to try to help this girl. "Why don't we go up to my office where we can chat more comfortably? We don't want to stand here in the lobby, do we?" She smiled warmly to reassure her and motioned toward the stairway.

The girl, suddenly eager, nodded and followed Lorna to her office. As soon as she was seated, tentatively, on the edge of a chair opposite Lorna's desk, she took a deep breath and asked, "What if I've done something wrong? What would you do?"

What could she have done, Lorna wondered, that would make her ask such a strange question? She hesitated only briefly before answering, hoping she would say the right thing and not frighten this girl into silence. "Suppose we talk about it a bit and then we'll decide what to do. The word *wrong* can mean many things, you know, and sometimes it helps to talk over your troubles with someone and see if things are really as bad as you think they are."

"Can I tell you anything—anything at all—and you won't be shocked, or tell anyone else, or try to make me do something I don't want to do?" The words tumbled out as the girl looked anxiously at Lorna.

The question was an awkward one, especially for an inexperienced social worker, but Lorna concealed her own uneasiness behind a kind, friendly smile. "I won't be shocked, and I'll respect your confidence if it is at all possible to do so. After all, you wouldn't want to make *me* promise anything that *you* wouldn't promise, would you?" Receiving an uncertain nod, Lorna continued. "Lots of girls come here to ask for advice or guidance, and we do everything we can that is legally permitted—to help them. But we don't try to force anyone to accept our advice, if they don't want it. So why not tell me what's troubling you?"

Her words seemed to have a reassuring effect for the girl leaned forward and said, almost in a whisper, "I've got to make up my mind about something. It's very important and

I haven't much time . . . I'm scared because—well, you see, I've run away."

Lorna suddenly realized that she was not surprised; something had warned her that this might be the case. But the situation was delicate, and her uneasiness increased as she tried to think of the best way to handle it. Before anything else, however, she had to have more facts. "Have you run away from home?" she said calmly.

"No—from Maple Lane. That's a reformatory, you know." The girl anxiously watched Lorna's face and seemed reassured that there was no expression of disapproval or shock. "I was home on a visit, and my father put me on the bus to go back. But when I got as far as Tacoma I suddenly decided that I couldn't go back *there* and got off at the bus station."

Lorna, of course, knew about the Girl's State Reformatory at Grand Mound and was aware that running away was a serious offense. She wished that there were someone older and wiser to turn to for advice, but she had to solve this problem by herself. To gain time, she asked, "If you're running away, what made you come here?"

"I don't know exactly. I've been walking around for hours, thinking about what I did. The more I thought, the less sure I was about what to do, where to go . . . Then I saw the Y.W.C.A. sign and remembered that, when I was a little girl, I was sent to a Y camp. I remembered how nice the lady counselor was"—her big brown eyes searched Lorna's face again—"she looked like you, a little, with pretty blonde hair and the bluest eyes . . . only you're much younger. Anyway, when I saw that sign, I came in . . ." Her voice trailed away into nothing and she looked even more lost and pathetic.

"You remembered that the blonde lady was a counselor—that was why you asked to speak to one?"

The girl nodded. Her teeth caught her lower lip, as if to

hold back tears. "That was the last nice summer I can remember. Just after that my mother died."

Lorna was deeply touched. Her uneasiness vanished, she had no thought of her eight-o'clock date. She only knew that she wanted to help this girl. After waiting a moment she said gently, "Would you like to tell me your name and a little more about yourself? I'll do whatever I can to help you."

The girl hesitated for an instant, then decided that she could trust her new-found friend. "I'm Glennie Ross. I live in Seattle—or I did until my father sent me away."

"Your father sent you?"

"Oh, I'd done something wrong. I was with some kids who stole a car. I had just learned to drive, but my father would never let me use our car. I thought it would be fun—I guess I just wasn't thinking. I'd have gotten off with a suspended sentence, but my father refused to be responsible for me. He was planning to get married again, and I was in the way, I suppose . . ."

"And did he remarry?"

"Yes." A hurt look came over Glennie's face and her eyes filled with tears. "She said she wouldn't marry him as long as I was around."

Lorna decided not to pursue that subject any further. "How old are you, Glennie?"

"Sixteen."

"How long must you stay at Maple Lane?"

"A year, if I go back. But I'm not going back!" She gripped the edge of the desk. "You promised you wouldn't make me do anything I didn't want to."

"I have no intention of doing that," Lorna replied. But somehow, she thought, she'd have to find a way to persuade Glennie that it was really best to return to the school. "I know a year seems a very long time, but what will you do if you don't go back?"

"Well——" Glennie thought for a moment. "I've been taking business classes. I can type." Then she added, "At least a little."

"You have to type well to hold a job."

"I can be a waitress."

"You'd have to have a permit. But even if you could pass for eighteen"—looking at her Lynn knew that she couldn't—"there would always be the danger that someone might recognize you. And when they found you, it would probably mean serving additional time."

"They wouldn't find me!"

"They usually do. You see, Glennie, when you are making a decision you must try to look at all sides of the problem. If you go back now, you can complete your business classes. Then you will be qualified to hold a job when you leave Maple Lane and you'll have no reason to be afraid."

"You want me to go back! I knew you would!" Glennie snatched up her overnight bag and started for the door. Lorna' first impulse was to stop her, but instinctively she knew that she must not. She forced herself to remain seated, but she wondered what to do if Glennie did run out of the building and disappear.

At the door, the girl looked back at Lorna with an expression of surprise and puzzlement. "You'd really let me go?" she asked unbelievingly.

"I told you I wouldn't try to force you to do anything you didn't want to do."

Glennie slowly moved back to her chair. She was so frightened and confused; long moments passed before she looked up at Lorna. "But you think—I should go back."

"Perhaps, but that doesn't matter. Regardless of what *I*

think, you have to make up your own mind," Lorna answered. She hoped that this was the right approach, knowing that she had to find some way—without seeming to do so—that would lead Glennie to the decision to go back. "Tell me something: do you play checkers?" Glennie nodded. "You see," Lorna continued, "making decisions is something like making moves in checkers. You have to think ahead, to see where the next step will take you. If you jump hastily, just because the way seems clear, you may leave yourself open for the opponent to take several men at once, and you will lose the game. But if you think out each play carefully, you have a far better chance of winning. Don't you agree?"

"I suppose so," Glennie said grudgingly, "but life isn't a game of checkers."

Lorna could hardly deny that the girl was right. However, she gave no sign of weakening her argument. "Of course not —life is a very serious business, which is all the more reason for making decisions much more carefully. But I'm sure you understood the point I was trying to make, even if you chose to ignore it." Lorna looked directly at Glennie, who began to show a sheepish smile.

"Yes, I knew . . . I was afraid you were trying to trap me. I guess you're not though." There was a long pause. The would-be runaway was staring thoughtfully at the floor. Finally she looked up. "I guess if I had thought ahead, I would not have gotten into trouble and been sent away."

Lorna had not meant that, but it did apply there too, so she merely nodded. "I was thinking more of the present—and the future. By going back now, you would be the winner in the long run."

"I never thought of it that way. Maybe you're right . . ." Glennie was wavering but not quite ready to accept the idea of returning to Maple Lane. "But I just can't bear the thought of waiting one whole year before I get out of that place."

Lorna leaned forward. "I know that sixteen seems very grown up to you and that a year can seem like a terribly long time, but it's not *forever*, Glennie. You can use that time to study hard, prepare yourself for a job. That's what you would do in any school, you know. And part of being grown up is being able to make the best of a situation, even if it's not an easy one. Tell me," she continued encouragingly, "what is it that you want out of life? Have you thought much about that?"

"I've thought about it, Miss Evans, but I don't know . . . any more. I used to think I wanted a home"—she looked up shyly—"but what can a girl who's been in a reformatory expect? It's not exactly something to boast about, and not everybody is as nice as you are about it."

"No, perhaps not everybody—but your own attitude is more important than anybody else's. You can expect what you are willing to work for." Lorna thought of Lisa Landon, one of the girls who was living at the Residence. "Would it help you to know that there is a girl here who came to us straight from Maple Lane two years ago because she had no place else to go? We helped her find a job and she's doing fine."

Glennie showed her surprise. "Do . . . the other girls here know about her?"

"Her closest friends do, though I'm sure it wouldn't matter in any case. Lisa has proved herself to be a very kind, good person, and that's what counts."

It was clear that hearing about Lisa had impressed and encouraged Glennie. "Could I come back here—I mean, when I'm through?"

"If you prepare yourself for a job, I'm sure we could help you find one."

"Could I—could I have a little time to think this over? Alone, I mean."

Lorna rose at once. "Of course. I'll wait in the hall. Call me when you're ready." On her way out she paused. "And remember that your *entire* future will depend on this decision, Glennie."

As she left the room Lorna wondered if there were anything more she should have said, but decided that it would have been unwise to push any more than she had. She glanced up at the hall clock. Six-thirty. She probably would not even have time to eat before Farley arrived. But she was not sorry that she had stayed.

A few moments later her office door opened. "I'm ready, Miss Evans." After they were both seated again, the girl took a deep breath. "I've decided. I'd go back, but I have no money."

"But you have a bus ticket——" Lorna stopped abruptly. Of course, the driver had collected it. But it occurred to her that Glennie might not really intend returning to the reformatory. In the next instant the girl intercepted that thought.

"You're thinking if I had the money I wouldn't go back."

"There's always that possibility," Lorna said with a smile, "but I trust you if you say you're going back."

"I wish *I* was sure I could trust myself. I didn't mean to run away when I left Seattle. The idea came on me suddenly. Maybe I'll do the same thing again . . ." Once more her face was troubled, frightened. "Would you ride with me to Grand Mound? To be sure I get there? I can't explain it, but somehow I feel *solid* with you."

"I'm sorry, Glennie, I wish I could, but I really can't." Lorna told herself it was impossible; yet would she go if it weren't for the party tonight? If it weren't for Milli Mercer?

"It's too long a trip and I have to be here tomorrow morning," she added quickly, smiling at Glennie and suppressing a guilty pang. "Anyway, I have a feeling you can trust yourself. You didn't really run away, you know. You came here." Reaching in the pocket of her coat she took out her purse and handed the girl a five-dollar bill. "I'll lend you the money for your fare."

"You do trust me!" Glennie's gratitude was embarrassing. "At one point I was afraid you'd call my father to take me back. Oh thank you! I'll pay you back. I have ten dollars saved at school. Honest, I'll send it to you."

"I know you will."

Glennie put the money in her worn pocketbook and picked up the bag. "Well, thank you again. Thank you very much. Good-by, Miss Evans."

Moments after the girl had walked out of the office, Lorna followed without knowing exactly why, and saw her standing at the top of the stairs, forlorn and irresolute.

"Glennie," Lorna called. "Wait a moment." She glanced at her watch. It was almost seven. "I'll drive you to the bus station."

Glennie's face brightened. "Oh would you? Really? Isn't it too much trouble?"

Lorna, moved by her eager, happy expression, said that it was no trouble at all. They walked downstairs and Mrs. Whitney called out good night as they crossed the lobby.

Once in the small gray Volkswagen, Glennie seemed to sink down and disappear into her too-big coat. Lorna glanced at her. "When did you eat last?" she asked.

"At noon, but I'm not hungry, really."

"Well, I am. I think I'll have a snack at the station."

Later, Glennie was still protesting that she didn't want anything to eat as Lorna ordered soup, hot turkey sandwiches, and milk and pie for both of them. She was pleased and

• 17

secretly amused to see that everything put in front of the girl quickly vanished.

"Oh, I feel so much better now," Glennie said as she finished the last bite of apple pie. "I *was* hungry—but you'd done so much for me already, I felt funny about letting you do any more. I don't know how to thank you."

"Just study hard and be patient and brave, that's the best thanks anybody could ask for," Lorna replied. "Come along now; it's almost seven-thirty and the bus will be here."

Lorna waited until Glennie was boarding the bus. Just as she was about to get in, she turned around. "You've been wonderful, Miss Evans. I'll never forget you, never."

"And I won't forget you, Glennie. I'd like to hear from you—will you write me and let me know how things are going?"

"Will I? I sure will! I wanted to ask you if I could, but I thought you might not like me to. Will you answer?"

"Of course I will. And if you can, call me tomorrow—but I know you'll be all right. You've made the right decision, and I'm proud of you."

Glennie smiled uncertainly and hurried aboard before the tears came. Lorna caught a last glimpse of her, face pressed against the window, as the bus rolled away. Would she really be all right? Lorna shivered and pulled her coat collar closer around her neck as the momentary doubt seized her. But it was too late to worry about it now. She had done the best she could.

Chapter Two

Lorna hurried out of the station and got into her car, telling herself that she'd be lucky to reach the apartment before Farley arrived. Well, at least she had telephoned her roommate Nola to say that she'd be late. What a blessing to have a friend who was thoughtful enough to say, "Don't worry about a thing. I've tidied up the place a bit, so all you'll have to do is make yourself pretty for that man of yours!"

Nola had graduated from the School of Social Work the year before Lorna, and she was now a social worker in the Children's Division of the Pierce County Welfare Agency. It was she who had written Lorna four months before about the opening on the Y.W.C.A. staff, and had also been of such great help to her in getting settled in Tacoma.

It was Nola, too, who had introduced Lorna to Farley Knowles on her second night in the new city. Peter Huston, a young police lieutenant in charge of the Youth Guidance Department, had invited both girls out for dinner, and Farley had come over to their table. The two men had played on the same high school basketball team and were still friends—although, as Peter laughingly said, they scarcely traveled in the same social circles.

Lorna had never known anyone like Farley Knowles. He was rich, handsome, intelligent, charming, and did everything with a flair. From that very first evening he had been attracted to her and she, in turn, was completely overwhelmed by this sudden development in her life. Was this really Lorna Evans—who had always been too busy studying to date very much—now being escorted everywhere by the most eligible bachelor in Tacoma, driving around with him in his black and silver Coupe de Ville, dining with him in the most elegant restaurants, dancing in his arms and feeling his lips brushing her hair, her cheek? She could hardly believe that all this was happening to her. But it was—and she loved every minute of it.

There were moments, though, when she had to admit to herself that she had doubts about their relationship. As she drove home now, she knew that Farley would not understand about Glennie. He had told her many times that she was too wrapped up in her work, that she gave too much of herself to the job. Well, perhaps she could not expect him to understand. Coming from a wealthy family, never having seen poverty and suffering, what did he really know about the heartaches of underprivileged, troubled children, who had little hope of making a better life for themselves unless people like herself and Nola and Peter tried to help them? She had tried to explain these things to Farley and, because he was basically kind and generous, she hoped that he would gradually come to realize the importance of her work.

Usually he treated the whole subject lightly, making some comment like, "When we're married, I'll be your full-time job!" Or he'd try to convince her that some extra duty or work, which often came unexpectedly her way and she felt obligated to attend to—as with Glennie—was less important than going to a concert or a play. More and more she was finding it hard to say no to his coaxing and pleas to go here, go there, do this, do that.

One night she had mentioned it to Nola, saying, "I guess I'm just too weak to resist his charm."

"Don't be silly," her friend had replied. "You're doing a wonderful job at the Y—even the Executive Director told me so last week when I spoke to her on the phone. Everyone is very impressed with your abilities and the interest you take in your work. Frankly, I think you're being too hard on yourself, Lorna. Why shouldn't you go out as much as you can with Farley?"

"It's just that I'm afraid that all these dates will interfere with my . . . career." Lorna had felt a little silly using that word, but Nola nodded in understanding.

"I know how you feel, and I sometimes ask myself the same questions you do. But neither of us has to worry about that *yet*."

"Well," Lorna said to herself now as she pulled up in front of the apartment building, "it may not solve anything, but it's certainly nice to have someone like Nola to talk to." Relieved to see that Farley's car was not already there, she ran inside and used the stairs, not bothering to wait for the elevator.

"Hi," she called as she opened the door.

"Hi yourself." Nola's dark head appeared from the kitchenette. "Glad you finally got here. I've got hot soup on."

"You're a honey, but I haven't got time. Anyway, I had a bite to eat a little while ago. I have to hurry now or I won't be ready when Farley comes." She had less than ten minutes to get ready.

"Farley won't *like* that!" Nola came into the living room and sank down on the ottoman, stretching her long legs in front of her. She had a stunning figure and beautiful classic features, with high, smooth cheekbones and dark, expressive eyes that were almost violet-blue. The willowy grace of her movements added to her striking appearance.

Lorna hung her tweed coat in the hallway closet and dashed into the bedroom. "I'm going to shower," she called. "Make an excuse to Farley if he gets here before I'm out, please."

"Will try."

She was out of the shower in minutes and searching for stockings in the drawer when Nola came in. "Can I help?"

"Get my dress, that's a darling."

"The new one?"

"Yes, I bought it especially for the party tonight."

Nola found the dress, a pale, pale green silk. She laid it on the bed.

Just then the doorbell rang. Lorna reached hastily for the dress. "Would you answer it, please? And go heavy on the charm to distract Farley!"

As she slipped the dress over her head, it ruffled her blonde hair, and she quickly ran the comb through it, allowing it to curl naturally about her face. Leaning forward at the dressing table to put her lipstick on, she stared at her reflection, noting the soft curve of her mouth, the vulnerable look on her face. "I guess I've fallen for the guy," she said to the girl in the mirror.

A light tap of the powder puff on her nose, two quick dabs of Farley's favorite perfume behind her ears, and she stood up to survey herself critically. The dress had the tiniest of cap sleeves, the wide neckline revealed the curve of her shoulders, the subtle draping of the silk molded the skirt attractively to her slim figure.

Farley rose as she entered the living room, and his face registered approval of what he saw.

"I'm sorry to be late, Farley, but something came up at the Y——"

"Tell me in the car, sugar." He held up her wrap. "We really have to be going." And with that he piloted her firmly to the door, giving a backward wave to Nola who called out, "Have fun."

In the car, when Farley looked at her, Lorna thought he was going to kiss her. Instead, he glanced at his watch, grinned at her, and started the car. Once they were on their way, his free hand found hers and she moved closer to him, glancing up at his face as she did so. He had a wonderful profile, a high forehead, thick dark hair. His hands were strong, yet graceful; his clothes were always well cut and made him look even more attractive. He turned briefly toward her.

"I didn't mean to be abrupt back there," he said, "but Marianne is furious if anyone is late to her parties."

"We *will* be late, and it's my fault."

"You take your work too seriously, sugar."

There it was again. Would he ever change? "It isn't that, Farley, but emergencies do arise. You can't just walk out on them."

"Let someone else handle them. There's a desk clerk, isn't there?"

"Mrs. Whitney isn't trained to handle problems—even if she had the time."

"Then they should have someone who can. They can't expect you to work all hours."

"We've been through all this before. Please try to understand: the Y is short-staffed. We have to operate on United Good Neighbor funds, and there never seems to be enough money. Surely you understand these business problems." Lorna was faintly annoyed but tried to keep the impatience out of her voice. "I wasn't late tonight—or on any other date —deliberately, you know. It's just that I couldn't ignore what I consider my responsibility, even if . . . even if it meant that I had to miss this party!"

"Well, it must have been *quite* an emergency." Farley sounded annoyed too. "Or perhaps this party isn't important to you."

"Let's not be childish about it," Lorna said, more gently. "*You* are important to me. And as for the party—I bought this dress especially for the occasion."

Farley squeezed her hand and smiled. It was his silent answer and Lorna felt relieved. They had never really quarreled before and this conversation was the nearest she ever wanted to come to it. Nevertheless, she had to try to make him see what she meant.

"Honestly, dear, if I hadn't tried to help that girl tonight, I don't know what might have happened to her." She briefly recounted Glennie's story, stressing the girl's despair and confusion, and ended by pointing out that the girl herself had made the decision to return to the reformatory.

But when Lorna finished, Farley grinned at her. "And you gave her five bucks?"

"Of course. Wouldn't you?"

"You mean you really think she intended to go back?"

"I can't be absolutely sure of it, but I had to take that chance. Glennie needed someone to believe in her. Letting her know that I trusted her was worth more than five dollars, believe me."

"You're an idealist, sugar," Farley said with a slight shrug.

"And you're cynical! I prefer to stay the way I am. I believe in such things as human decency and kindness." In spite of her desire to avoid argument, she was angered by his indifferent attitude.

"I suppose I am cynical—you can't be in business without becoming a bit jaundiced about people." His voice had softened, and he put his arm around her and gave her a quick hug. "I love you for your faith in humanity, sugar."

She leaned against him, her anger gone. This, she knew, amounted to an apology. She supposed that Glennie's story did sound incredible to him. Many things a social worker hears and sees would seem unbelievable to most people. The experiences he had in his business, the largest men's shop in Tacoma, doubtless gave him a quite different kind of perspective on life. Anyway, this was no time for arguing; the sky was like blue velvet, the stars seemed low enough to touch.

There were a lot more people at the party than Lorna had expected; some she didn't know at all. Several of Farley's friends gathered around as they came in, and Marianne playfully scolded Farley for being late. While they were standing there, Milli Mercer came up to join them. Lorna would have recognized her from the description she had been given, even if Milli hadn't thrown her arms around Farley.

Farley returned the embrace for a moment, then released her. "Europe hasn't changed you," he said, laughing.

"And you haven't changed, darling," she gurgled, tucking her hand under his arm. More people came up, and suddenly Lorna found herself out at the edge of the group.

"I'm glad to be home," said Milli.

"It will seem tame," Farley replied.

"*I* don't think so." She gave him a lingering smile.

The expression "golden girl" passed through Lorna's mind; she vaguely recalled reading it somewhere. Milli was exactly that. Her blonde hair was swept up modishly from the tips of her ears into a Grecian knot, with a few golden tendrils curling gracefully against her slender neck. The sophisticated elegance of the hair style made Lorna's casual curls seem childish. Milli's skin was truly golden, not browned from the summer's swimming like Lorna's. Her expensive dress, the shade of cream-colored roses, had gold threads woven into the material. Her eyes were not blue, as one might have expected, but a deep brown in startling contrast to her hair.

Lorna must have been frowning, for a young man near her said. "Don't let it bother you."

His words startled her.

"It doesn't mean anything," he said. "It's just Milli's way of blowing up a storm." He was smiling at her. Both the flickering smile and the thoughtful gray eyes were pleasantly at ease and friendly.

"I'm Greg Taylor. I've been away."

"I'm Lorna Evans. I've just arrived."

"I know. Farley's an old friend of mine. He wrote me about you." His voice was rich and deep; Lynn liked the sound of it.

At that moment Farley came over to them. "I see you two have met." He put a hand on Greg's shoulder. "This is my old pal, Lorna. We grew up together."

Milli suddenly appeared next to Farley. "I haven't met your Lorna." She clasped her small hands around his arm, looking pertly at the other girl. "Oh!" she cooed. "She's gorgeous! Why didn't someone tell me?" She turned her radiance on them all, then looked slyly at Lorna. "But I thought you'd be wearing a gray dress with a high collar, and be as pious as my Aunt Louise."

The remark threw Lorna off balance. Was this girl being deliberately cruel? She's soft as a kitten, she decided, and you don't see the tiny claws until they dig into you. Aloud she said, "You've got me mixed up with a New England Puritan, I'm afraid."

"You've been away too long, Milli." Greg Taylor spoke

quietly. "Social workers don't wear high white collars any more."

Lorna felt Farley take her arm. "You must meet Marianne's mother," he said, drawing her away in an effort to smooth over the situation.

It seemed to Lorna, later, that he spent most of his time rescuing her, for whenever Milli sought her out—and she did repeatedly—Farley would appear. It gave Lorna the uncomfortable feeling that he did not think she could cope with Milli . . . and she had to admit she had not done too well in the first encounter. Yet, Milli also managed to be near Farley a great deal of the time. She had a way of standing very close to him, hanging onto his every word, gazing up at him in a wide-eyed, possessive way. But on the whole the evening went fairly well—until they were just about to leave.

Lorna was talking with Mary Renlo, a talented artist and one of the people she liked best in Farley's crowd. The party was breaking up and Farley had already gotten her wrap. She asked him if he would mind waiting a few more minutes because she was discussing arrangements with Mary, who had volunteered to conduct an art class at the Y. Farley strolled over to the fireplace around which a small group of guests still lingered.

After finishing her talk with Mary, Lorna walked over to join him, and as she approached, she heard Milli say, "She didn't really, not really!"

"That's a fiver Lorna will never see again," Jerry Lester hooted.

"That's what I told her," Farley said. He turned then and saw her. "I was explaining why we were late—Marianne wanted to know."

Lorna was speechless with anger. Farley knew how she felt about respecting her confidences. She was hurt, too, to think that he would make light of something that meant so much to her. "I don't know what Farley has told you," she said through tight lips, "but five dollars isn't much to invest in a girl's chance for a future. And the money itself is not the real issue."

"Do you do that sort of thing often?" asked Jerry, apparently missing the point. "I suspect you do."

"Not as often as I'd like," was Lorna's only reply.

"You really are naïve, my dear," Milli said languidly. "You ought to travel more—you'd learn a lot about people."

"I'm afraid I can't afford that luxury," Lorna answered, wondering why she bothered to explain to these people how she felt. "But five dollars won't break me, and I'll gladly give money whenever I feel it will help, even if I don't get it back. However, in this case I think the money *will* be returned."

Marianne Blakely burst out laughing. "Stop kidding yourself, Lorna! You'll never see that five bucks again!"

Lorna looked at her coolly, but before she could say anything, Greg Taylor spoke up.

"She'll get it back." He was sitting on the couch a few feet away, but his quiet voice carried conviction and made everyone turn to look at him. Marianne, who had been in his shadow most of the evening, walked over to him and curled up at his side, but she did not contradict him.

Lorna studied Greg for a moment, listening to the others' protests and doubts—as if it mattered to them, she thought. Finally she asked, "What makes you say she'll return the money, Greg?"

"He's a soft touch too," Farley replied for his friend, giving him an amused but affectionate look.

"He's one of you," Milli put in. "You know, a social worker," she added as Lorna stared blankly.

"I'm with the Child Guidance Clinic," Greg explained.

"I thought you knew. I just came here from Minneapolis."

Lorna smiled. "I'm very glad you're 'one of us,'" she said, ignoring Milli's half-amused, half-annoyed shrug.

At the door Lorna turned to her hostess. "Thank you for the nice evening. I'm sorry I made Farley late. I'll try not to let it happen again." If she sounded politely sarcastic, she didn't care.

In the car, she sank back against the seat, shivering slightly with the cold. She was aware that Farley glanced over at her several times, but she did not look at him. Remembering that dejected expression on Glennie's face as she gazed out the bus window, Lorna felt unhappy, and angry at the people at Marianne's party.

Lorna's face must have reflected her emotions, for finally Farley said, "I hope you're not upset about what happened back there."

"Frankly I am," she replied flatly. "What made you tell them? They could never understand such things, and you know that I am not supposed to discuss cases. I thought you'd respect my confidence, even if you aren't sold on the idea of social work."

"Oh, come off it, sugar." Farley sounded aggravated too. "I didn't tell them anything important—I don't even know the kid's last name. All I said was that a girl had conned you out of five bucks with some hard-luck story."

"*Conned?* That's an ugly word, Farley, and there's no excuse for your using it. You're as bad as they are. Maybe if you had met Glennie, you would never have said that. But I never should have told you about it. That was my real mistake." Her distress was justified, because she knew of cases where there were unfortunate consequences as a result of divulging confidences. But it was best to drop the subject.

Apparently Farley had decided to drop it too, for his next

remark came as a surprise to Lorna: "What did you think of my friend Greg? He's quite a guy, isn't he?"

Lorna replied that she could hardly have much of an impression after so brief a meeting, but she added that she found him very likable and considerate. "What made him decide to do social work?" she asked.

"Search me. He could have been anything he wanted to be; his family is one of the richest in Tacoma. But you'd never know it, would you?" The admiration in his voice was unconcealed. "Old Greg really has talent too."

"You sound as if social work doesn't require talent," Lorna told him defensively.

"Oh, for heavens' sake, sugar, I didn't mean that. I was thinking about the money——"

"Money isn't everything!" she interrupted.

Farley grinned at her. "You can't deny that it helps," he drawled. "You're deliberately trying to pick a fight with me tonight, sugar, but I won't let you get away with it. Just let me finish my sentences before you jump to conclusions. Greg has always been a dreamer. If he had wanted to serve humanity, he could have become a doctor."

"When will you learn that a social worker serves humanity too? Helping people with their problems is as important as giving medical care. You seem to think that a person is a dreamer if he chooses social work as a career, but you're wrong. Nothing could be more down-to-earth than the problems a social worker has to face every day in his job. He sees the hard, cruel realities of life and must try to bring comfort and help to people in trouble. That's why I did what I did today."

"Look, Lorna, that five dollars you gave was your money. Being you, there was nothing else you could do but give it. I won't argue that point."

Lorna studied him reproachfully. "But you still think it was foolish of me to do it. Well, let me tell you something. I should have gone with her to Maple Lane when she asked me to, instead of going to that party. If anything happens to that girl, I'll never forgive myself, never." A tear rolled down her cheek and she brushed it away impatiently.

They had just reached her apartment building, and Farley pulled the car under the shadowing branches of a large tree. After switching off the motor he drew her into his arms. "I hate to see you getting so worked up, honey. I didn't mean to upset you, but you take these things too seriously. You've got to learn to be more objective about these cases. And stop worrying about Glennie; she'll be all right."

"I hope so," Lorna whispered, her voice muffled against his shoulder. "I didn't mean to fight with you, truly I didn't. Let's not ever be angry with one another again. . . ."

His lips silenced hers, and she lost herself in his kiss. And later, when she quietly stole into the bedroom, tiptoeing about so she wouldn't wake Nola, she asked herself how she had been so lucky as to meet Farley. No one had ever mattered so much to her. When he put his arms around her, the whole world disappeared.

But after she got into bed and pressed her cheek against the cool pillow, the world was no longer shut out, and she could not shut out the thoughts that returned to bother her. It was true, she admitted to herself in the dark: she did take things too seriously. She did worry about her job, the people who came to her for help. But there was more to it. She didn't understand Farley and his friends—not really. She could far more easily understand someone like Glennie, who had so little, because she herself had had so little. That was the basic difference between them, and perhaps it could never be overcome.

Having always seen the sober side of life, she had accepted it as natural, inevitable, until she met Farley. A new and carefree existence suddenly had become possible, and it was tempting and exciting. Could she slowly adopt that new point of view? Had she not begun to do so already, without realizing it? Admittedly, her clothes were smarter, her interests had broadened, her enjoyment in life had increased. But the question was: Could she change enough to compete with Milli? And more important, did she want to change that much?

She could still see Milli flirting openly with Farley in front of all their friends, making it clear to everyone that she had by no means given him up and intended to win him back somehow.

I *won't* let her take him away from me, Lorna resolved, turning on her side and pulling the covers up around her neck. And I won't let her keep me awake. She closed her eyes, but it wasn't easy to get rid of the image of the mocking, smiling "golden girl."

Chapter Three

At her office before eight-thirty the next morning, Lorna found a letter from her parents on her desk. As she read it, she missed them both terribly.

Mr. Evans, coming from Wales as a young man, had married early and had worked all his life in a mill in Seattle. Feeling his lack of education keenly, he had been determined to send his son and daughter to school so they would not have to labor the way he had. Nels, who was fifteen years older than Lorna, had become a chemist and was now living with his wife and family in California. Mr. Evans was proud of his two children and had given them encouragement and assurance during the years of their schooling. Throughout the many hardships and struggles, they had remained a close and loving family.

Lorna's mother had worked in a cannery for many years, but in spite of the long hours at her job, she had never failed anyone who called on her for help. And call they did, for many of the families in their neighborhood were very poor. Their need was so great that Mrs. Evans had offered her services at the nearby Community House, where she taught sewing, cooking, and helped in whatever way she could. As people came to know and trust her, they turned to her in time of sickness or trouble and they were never disappointed.

As Lorna grew older, she, too, had helped, and it was then that she saw and felt the need to give people kindness and care and listen to their problems. Perhaps her mother gave too much of herself, and suffered with the needy and the poor more than she should have; but Lorna only knew that the need was great and that her mother was too kind-hearted to refuse to give it. It was only when her father retired the year before and decided to accept Nels' invitation to spend the winter with him that her mother had stopped going to the Community House and answering the many demands made on her. Lorna knew that her father's pension was very small and she was relieved that her parents could get away for a winter and have a well-earned rest.

"Busy?" A honey-blonde head appeared in Lorna's office doorway. "Or daydreaming?"

Lorna smiled and beckoned Bea Miller in. "Daydreaming, I'm afraid. How about some coffee to wake me up?"

"I have some all ready." The other girl disappeared back into the adjoining office. She was a godsend to the Y, which normally could not have afforded another person, but Bea had been willing to work for whatever salary the Y could pay her. Her mother had fallen sick and she had been forced to interrupt her last year of graduate school in social work in order to return home and assume family responsibilities. Her father was dead and there were two younger sisters who were in school. Bea had a wonderfully calm and sunny disposition, which made her well liked at the Y, and she had done very well in handling the Y-teen groups under Lorna's direction.

She returned to Lorna's office with a coffee pot and two cups. "This will wake *both* of us up!" They exchanged smiles and sipped the steaming brew in silence for a few moments. "I was wondering if you would come to the Y-teen meeting tonight, Lorna?" Bea asked. "We're planning the fall dance and I'd like to have your opinions on some of the points that will be brought up. Besides, the girls always love to have you around."

"I'll be glad to, Bea, but I'll be a little late. Mary Renlo is beginning her art class tonight and I have to be on hand for that first. Anyway, you don't need my opinions—you're doing a terrific job with the group."

Bea smiled. "Thank you for those kind words, Lorna. You have no idea how grateful I am for the experience I'm getting here. This job proves to me that group work is my field." They discussed some of the events for the following week over a second cup of coffee, then Bea picked up the tray. "Well, back to work. Oh, by the way, I saw Mae Devlin on the way this morning and she asked me to have you drop by her office when you have a few minutes free today."

Lorna got up. "I'll go now. If I get a phone call from Grand Mound, be sure to have it transferred—it'll be important." She had been hoping for a call from Glennie and was beginning to imagine all kinds of things that might have happened to the girl.

Mae Devlin was the Executive Director of the Y.W.C.A., and Lorna admired the older woman a great deal for her wisdom and gentleness. The staff in general was a small and congenial group, and the work was divided among them on an elastic basis, with duties sometimes overlapping departmental divisions. Jo Nordy had charge of the Health and Recreation Program; Ruth Larkin was in charge of the business management. Lorna had less contact with them than with Miss Devlin and Mrs. Hart, the Residence Housemother.

The Executive Director acted as counselor for the girls who lived at the Y, although they often took their minor troubles to Mrs. Hart. In spite of her many duties involving housekeeping supervision, the Housemother always found time if any of the forty resident girls sought her help.

Recently, Mae had asked Lorna to assist her in the counseling because the load was a heavy one, and had referred several cases to her. Of late, she had considered counseling the most challenging aspect of her job, and as she neared Mae's office she began to wonder if her work had been unsatisfactory. She tapped nervously on the closed door and entered the Executive Director's office with thumping heart.

"Good morning, my dear, I'm glad you were able to drop in so early. I was anxious to talk to you as soon as possible." Mae had held her position for many years and was an extremely observant and sensitive person. "I hope you haven't been worried about the reason for this visit," she added. "You have no need to be."

"Well, I guess I was a little nervous," Lorna admitted with a shy smile.

"I have a favor to ask, my dear—although it means more work for you, I'm afraid." It was like Mae to come directly to the point. "I went to my doctor last week and he told me that I must slow down for a little while. It's nothing serious, if I follow his advice now. However, the only way I can do so is to cut down my work load by turning over the Residence counseling to someone else." Picking up a pencil, Mae made a few small spirals on the pad in front of her, then looked up at Lorna. "That someone is you, my dear. I know that your own work has kept you very busy, and we are especially pleased with the new classes and groups you have organized. If you are willing, we will reorganize things a bit, giving Bea more responsibility. You've reported that she has done very well, so I think she could handle the teen-agers and a few other duties, to free you for the counseling."

"Bea and I can figure something out, I'm sure, and I'll be glad to help in any way I can."

Mae put down the pencil. "What I have in mind is for you to take over *all* of the Resident counseling, Lorna."

Lorna could hardly believe her ears, and she could think of nothing to say as the implications of the new job dawned on her. She had had training in counseling in school, of course, but her actual experience was so limited that she had never dreamed of being asked to take on the whole load.

Considering the fact that the forty girls who lived at the Y came from varying backgrounds and were of different races and religions, it was not surprising that some of the counseling problems were not easy to handle. Most of the residents were average, healthy young women who had taken jobs away from home, but there were, from time to time, a few whose unhappy lives in earlier years had left scars and created serious difficulties for them. Since they could not always cope with their problems and adjust to new people and situations, it was an important function of the Y to try and help them toward a happier, fuller and Christian way of life.

It was a big job—and Lorna was not at all sure that she could cope with it.

As if in answer to her unspoken doubts, the Executive Director said, "I'll always be available whenever you want to discuss something, and naturally you can count on Mrs. Hart. She's been of invaluable help to me." Mae smiled at her assistant. "She's an instinctively wise and amazingly perceptive woman, you know. Perhaps you need some time to think this over. I don't want to place more responsibility on you than you are ready to accept, my dear."

Lorna hesitated. "Do you think I could do a good job?"

"If I didn't think so, I wouldn't suggest this arrangement to you. It's too important a job. As a matter of fact, I've been wondering why you didn't choose counseling as your specialty—you'd done so well with the cases I've sent you."

"I suppose I don't feel sure enough of myself to advise others," Lorna began, then hastily added, "but I have enjoyed the work so much that I'd like to continue it."

Mae considered Lorna's first remark. "You don't really *advise* in the sense of telling people what to do, as you well know. Your function is to listen, ask a few questions, and point out things that someone who is troubled may have overlooked or been unaware of. In doing this, you clarify the issues, bring a perspective to the problem that the person has lacked. You help them restore confidence in themselves, and once they are sure of their inner strength, you are able to help them examine the possible solutions and guide them along constructive paths—they themselves must make the final decision." Mae nodded wisely. "You'd be surprised how often they are able to make the right one. People usually know what's best for them—all they need is the patient understanding and encouragement of someone they trust. So it turns out that you are helping them to help themselves."

Lorna smiled gratefully. "Which is what you are doing with me right now," she replied, and Mae returned the smile. "I'm willing to try, although I know I still have a lot to learn."

"That's my girl." The way Mae leaned back and relaxed in her chair told Lorna that her acceptance of the new work had eased the older woman's mind considerably.

"It's odd, but something that happened last night, just as I was leaving here, proves exactly what you've just been saying to me." Lorna quickly outlined Glennie's situation and the outcome of their meeting. "Perhaps it was not wise to lend her the money," she concluded, "but I'm not sorry I did."

Mae gave her an approving nod. "We must do what we feel is *right* at the moment, because we can never know for sure what is the *wisest*. No matter how excellent our training, we cannot be assured of success with every case. Furthermore, we rarely see the direct results of our efforts because effective counseling extends over a long period of time and cases pass out of our hands. In any event, we cannot afford to waste time dwelling on our failures—possible or otherwise—for there are too many who need our help." Mae paused, looking ruefully out the window for a moment. "We have all had our ups and downs, my dear, as well as self-doubts, but there's no room for discouragement in this field."

"You make me realize what a long way I have to go," Lorna told her, impressed with the woman's quiet strength. "I do have a tendency to want to do too much and see the results right away."

"You've come a long way already, Lorna. After all, it's been only—what?—four months? I have complete faith in you and you'll make a fine counselor."

Lorna felt a flush of pleasure on hearing those words from a person who did not give praise lightly, and she was determined to prove herself worthy of such confidence.

"We have a problem that you may as well begin with—and it won't be an easy one, I'm afraid," Mae said, looking at a sheet of paper covered with notes. "Reverend Marlow called me yesterday about a girl in his parish and is coming here today at one-fifteen to discuss the situation. I think I'll let you talk to him, rather than try to explain the case to you. I'll let you know when he arrives, and you two can get acquainted—I know you'll like each other and work together on other cases in the future." Mae stood up to indicate that the meeting was over. "Thank you very much, my dear. Your willingness to take on this new job makes me feel much better."

Lorna walked slowly back to her own office, feeling nervous at the prospect of facing her first case alone. It would take time to adjust to this unexpected development in her career. Here she was, less than a year out of school, and a whole new area was about to open to her—one that had always interested her. She was certainly fortunate that Mae Devlin was the kind of person who was willing to give newcomers a chance to grow, instead of getting a more experienced social worker to take over.

The distant tinkle of a telephone roused Lorna out of her thoughts, and she hurried her steps as she realized that it was hers. Maybe Glennie was calling . . .

"Hello, sugar." It was Farley's voice and momentarily she was disappointed. "Hope you're not busy tonight. Milli has asked a few of us to her house."

"I'm sorry but I can't make it . . ."

"What's the matter? Another girl in trouble?" His tone was light, but she knew he did not like to be refused.

"No, but Mary Renlo is starting a class tonight and I have to be here, and also drop in on another meeting after that."

"This overtime stuff is getting to be quite a habit—or do you work there twenty-four hours a day?" His voice was edged with annoyance.

Lorna let this remark pass. "We can always go another time, Farley. However, if it's that important, maybe you should go without me." She hoped that he would say no and offer to meet her later for a hamburger; but to her chagrin he said that he would do just that. After all, Milli was an old friend.

"So long, sugar, call you tomorrow," he hung up, leaving Lorna to stare at the dead receiver.

A short while later all thoughts of Farley and Milli's party were pushed aside as Lorna went down to meet Reverend Marlow, who turned out to be a kindly-looking man in his early fifties. As he spoke quietly to her, she began to learn some of the facts of the case he had come to ask help with. It turned out that the girl, Judy Stillman, was a seventeen-year-old whose mother was dead and whose father had taken her out of school last spring to keep house for him. The girl had gradually lost interest in everything and had become extremely withdrawn, to the point where she refused to leave the house at all. "Her only interest now is in the piano, which she plays beautifully," the minister concluded. "I feel we must get her away from that unhealthy atmosphere or she will have a breakdown."

"What do you think we might do for her?" Lorna asked.

"I think she should be removed from her home. I'd like to see her placed in the Y, where she would have the companionship of girls her own age, as well as the guidance of someone who would take a great deal of interest in her. Her mother's death was a severe blow and she needs love and proof of being wanted."

Lorna immediately thought of Mrs. Hart, whose motherly concern for the Residence girls had been a great asset to the Y on many occasions. "What's the matter with the father? Doesn't he see what's happening to his daughter?" she asked, not wanting to make any commitments until she knew more about the situation.

"Mr. Stillman was fifteen years older than his wife, and he hasn't the slightest idea of how to handle a child—especially a girl. He has been so severe in his demands on Judy, both at home and at school, that she feels as if everything she does is a failure. She was always such a sensitive child and eager to please, but now she's incapable of trying to do anything."

Lorna's first impulse had been to tell the minister to bring Judy to the Y at once, but she knew that there were many factors to consider before reaching such a decision. Many questions were racing through her mind, and some answers were necessary before she could act. Would the father permit his daughter to leave home in the first place? How would Judy adjust to new surroundings? Would she be able to fit in or would she feel even more unwanted and left out? Would she respond to the help that was offered her or was she too upset to accept it? She would have to learn some kind of work, so that she could eventually support herself and be independent. After all, she could not remain at the Y forever . . .

Lorna did not mention any of these things, but said instead, "I'm afraid Judy might find it hard to be here alone most of the day, although I suppose that could be handled if she were to come. Then there's the question of money. Will her father pay for her? If not, we might have to seek aid from one of the other agencies in town."

"I've thought about that, Miss Evans, and I'll try to get Mr. Stillman to contribute to her support. He claims that she's retarded and he'll have her on his hands all his life. I have discussed the girl with some of the teachers she had in school and they find no evidence to that effect. She did very well until her mother died five years ago. After that her record slumped, and I'm convinced that her grief and unhappiness at home were responsible for her poor showing in school." Reverend Marlow was silent for a few seconds.

"I'd appreciate your opinion, Miss Evans. Do you think she can be helped?"

My opinion! Lorna wondered how surprised the minister would be if he knew how uncertain she often felt about her counseling. Assuming her most professional air, however, she said, "At this point I really can't say. I think that I should first have a talk with Judy; after that I'll have a clearer impression of the situation. Then we can discuss it further. I can only tell you that, if possible, we will try to help this girl. When could I arrange to see her?"

Reverend Marlow glanced at his watch. "It's almost two now. Would it be convenient for you to pay a visit this afternoon? If so, we could go now."

Lorna was about to delay the meeting, so that she could discuss the case with Mae, but she caught herself in time. It would hardly be sensible or fair to go running to the Executive Director every time she started a case. She would have to make up her own mind and be responsible for her course of action, if she ever hoped to be of value as a counselor. Lorna stood up resolutely. When she had more facts, she could present the situation and her recommendation officially. "It would suit me perfectly, Dr. Marlow; the sooner the better. If you'll excuse me one moment, I'll get my coat and we can leave right away."

As they approached the Stillman house on the outskirts of the city, Lorna caught sight of a large pasture, a row of fruit trees, and a chicken house. It would have been a pleasing sight, except that the place had a neglected air about it.

There was no response to the minister's first rap on the front door, but upon his second knock it inched open just enough to permit a face to peep out timidly. The only features that Lorna could distinguish in the shadow were enormous dark eyes, doe-like and sad in a small white face. As the door opened wider, she could see that the girl who stood on the threshold was beautiful, with gleaming dark hair that hung down her back in rippling waves.

"Oh, it's you, Dr. Marlow." There was little inflection in her voice, but the solemn expression softened a little.

"Hello, Judy. I've brought a friend of mine to visit you. May we come in?"

The girl stepped back to let them enter, then silently guided them into the living room. She sat stiffly across from them, her face closed and remote.

The minister was gentle with her as he spoke. "Miss Evans is from the Y.W.C.A., Judy. Remember, I was telling you about it when I was here last time?"

"Yes, I remember. My mother used to take me there to swim in the pool." Her voice sounded very far away.

Lorna smiled at her. "Would you like to go there again?"

The answer came slowly, almost reluctantly. "I . . . think so, if I could . . ." She thought about it a little longer. "Yes, I'd like that."

Now the three of them were talking quietly, with Lorna and the minister prompting Judy to tell them things she liked or wanted to do. The girl seemed willing to talk, although her replies were guarded and hesitantly offered. Underneath her frozen exterior there was a flicker of warmth.

"I liked school," she volunteered at one point, "but my father thought it was a waste of time . . . I guess it was . . . I didn't do very well."

"Would you like to go back to school?" Lorna asked.

Judy motioned vaguely around the room. "There's all this housework . . ."

"How would you like to live at the Y?" Reverend Marlow asked. "Miss Evans thinks it would be a wonderful idea; so do I. Shall I ask your father to let you?"

Judy stared down at the carpet and traced out a design with the toe of one shoe. Just as Lorna had given up hope of an answer, the girl looked up. "Yes," she whispered, "I'd go, but . . . my father wouldn't let me."

The minister walked over to her and placed a gentle hand on her head. "We'll see, my dear, we'll see." Then he went to the piano and began to leaf through some music on the rack. "Oh, this is a lovely piece, Judy. Would you care to play it for us? I know Miss Evans would enjoy hearing it."

The girl rose obediently and joined Reverend Marlow. The instant her fingers touched the keys, all the sensitivity within her found expression in the notes. Lorna realized that Judy was lost in another world, enveloped in dreams that no one else could share, or destroy. The music and the musician were one.

Judy continued to play, piece after piece, until the chimes of a distant clock suddenly broke the spell and her hands faltered and dropped to her lap. "I must stop now," she murmured. "It's time to begin dinner."

"That was beautiful, Judy, more beautiful than anything I have ever heard," Lorna told her earnestly. "Thank you for sharing it with us."

The girl's eyes revealed how grateful she was for those words, but she did not reply.

Reverend Marlow turned at the front door. "Tell your father I'll be dropping by for a chat with him one evening very soon."

"It won't do any good—he doesn't want me to leave," Judy said despondently.

"You let me worry about that," the minister answered. "I'm sure we can work something out."

As they walked down the path Judy's voice came floating

after them, "Come back again, Miss Evans . . . please come back and see me."

Lorna's throat tightened, but she managed a smile as she turned around to wave. "I'll be seeing you *very* soon, I promise."

The slight figure was still outlined in the doorway as they drove away.

Chapter Four

"How long has this been going on?" Lorna asked when she had composed herself.

"Too long," Reverend Marlow replied grimly. "It's gotten worse gradually, as would be expected under the circumstances. Such a sweet, gifted child too."

"I suppose her father won't consult a doctor?" Lorna asked, knowing the answer already. "Well something must be done right away. I certainly hope Mr. Stillman listens to reason this time."

The minister gripped the steering wheel tightly. "I'll see to it that he does. If I have to, I'll take stern measures to protect that girl from further trouble."

Lorna did not press him to explain what he meant, but a sidelong glance at his determined jaw told her that he did not intend to take no for an answer.

"Do you think she can be admitted into the Residence, Miss Evans?"

"Naturally I have to discuss the matter with the staff, but I assure you that I will make a strong recommendation to have her accepted. I think it can be arranged, as long as we can be sure of having funds provided."

"I'm going to drop by the Child Guidance Clinic and see what Gregory Taylor has to say about that. I've known him since he was a lad, and I'm sure he'll do whatever he can to help. He'll know what resources are available for the purpose."

Gregory Taylor. Lorna recalled how nice he had been to her last evening. "I met him for the first time yesterday," she said. "He seems to be an unusual person."

"As a matter of fact, he is," Reverend Marlow agreed. "He has a deep interest in children, especially those who are troubled or are otherwise in need of special care. I attribute this to the fact that he himself was an adopted child."

Lorna could think of nothing to say. That possibility had never occurred to her, and although she was curious to hear more, she did not want to seem to be prying into such a personal matter.

The minister, however, apparently felt inclined to talk about it. "Mr. and Mrs. Taylor are people of fine character, who are more concerned with the good that money can do than with money itself," he said. "Mr. Taylor has always provided better wages and working conditions for his employees than many other businessmen, which has made him highly respected in Tacoma. . . . Well, here we are."

Reverend Marlow drew up to the curb and Lorna opened the door to get out. "Please call me when you have talked to Gregory," she requested, shaking the minister's hand. "Meanwhile I'll take care of things here."

"I'll see him as soon as possible, Miss Evans. And thank you for everything."

She ran up the steps, noting that it was already four o'clock, and paused at the desk in the lobby to ask if a call had come from Glennie, but there was no message for her. Disappointed and a little worried she continued upstairs to her office to check her afternoon mail. On her desk was a penciled note; it was from Mae Devlin.

Lorna: I have left for the day. If, after seeing the Stillman girl, you feel that she should be accepted here as a resident, go ahead and make arrangements with Mrs. Hart. I'm sure you two can work something out, provided expenses are covered. Just put your case report on my desk before you go home, so that I can look it over in the morning.

Good luck. Mae

Well, Lorna thought with pleasure, she's leaving this entirely up to me; she must really have confidence in my judgment.

Since there was no correspondence that required her immediate attention, she picked up a blank folder, labeled it *Stillman, Judy*, and headed for Mrs. Hart's small apartment in the Residence section of the building. A sign on the door read: *"Back in five minutes. Please wait inside,"* so Lorna went in. The living room was comfortable and homey, with photographs of Mrs. Hart's children, all married now, framed on the wall over a small spinet piano. A large assortment of books filled three shelves on the opposite wall. Lorna knew from former visits that the volumes included such topics as psychology, careers for women, religion, love and marriage. The Residence girls often dropped by to borrow one or another book and have a friendly chat with the Housemother. Gazing around at the cheerful, tidy place, Lorna could understand why they liked to come here.

A few minutes later Mrs. Hart returned and greeted her visitor warmly. She dropped into a nearby chair and sighed as she slipped her feet out of her shoes. "Well, Lorna, it's nice to see you again. I've just been checking up on one of the girls who's sick."

"You do have your hands full, Mrs. Hart. And I've come

to see if you can add one more lamb to your flock." Lorna told her about Judy Stillman, and was relieved to see the Housemother nodding sympathetically.

"Poor thing," she murmured when Lorna had finished. "We could squeeze her in somehow, even though the accommodations are a little cramped right now. How soon would she be arriving?"

"I expect to hear from Dr. Marlow in a day or two. As soon as he calls, I'll let you know if it's definite." She thought a moment, then added: "I think Judy would be better off in a room by herself, at least temporarily. If she is able to make friends with someone, perhaps she could move into a double room later on."

Mrs. Hart agreed. "After all you've told me about the situation, I suspect that it might take the girl a while to adjust to new surroundings. However, given love and attention, she can be drawn out of her shell."

"I hope you're right, and at least it's worth a try. If Judy does come, you'll be able to do a lot for her, I know—all the girls consider you a second mother."

A number of small chores that had piled up during the day now demanded Lorna's attention.

Even though she had little time to think of anything but the work in front of her, she was aware of a growing concern for Glennie Ross. Why hadn't the girl called? Had she not gone back to the reformatory after all? Lorna told herself not to worry, but it did no good. She wondered if she should try to call Maple Lane and find out if the runaway had returned . . . Then she decided against the idea.

When she glanced at the clock again, it was almost five. There seemed little chance of hearing from Glennie now, and fear seized her again. Suddenly the phone pealed sharply, and her hand shot out to pick up the receiver before the first ring ended.

"Yes?"

"Grand Mound calling," the operator said. "Just one moment, please."

"Hello, Miss Evans?" a hesitant voice asked. "This is Glennie. Glennie Ross. Remember me?"

"Of course I do. I was wondering if you were going to call."

"Well, I wanted to let you know I got here—at the school, I mean. They said I could call you."

"I'm so glad you did." That was a gross understatement indeed! "Are you all right?"

"Yes . . . I told them what happened . . . I don't think they liked it. But I'm back and I'm all right . . . About the money, Miss Evans—I'll send it to you."

"The money doesn't matter; the important thing is that you got back safely."

"You're swell, honest. I—I'll write you soon . . . I have to hang up now. Thank you . . . Good-by."

Lorna sat there, staring at the phone, letting the waves of relief wash over her. She had been right about Glennie! Almost before she was aware of her intention, she dialed Farley's office number.

"I just had to tell you," Lorna said as soon as he answered. "Glennie called. She *did* go back."

"Well, good for her, sugar."

She was disappointed that his reaction was so mild, but what else could she expect? He had not met the girl, so how could it really matter to him? "I guess you think I'm making a big thing out of this," she said half-apologetically.

"It's not that, Lorna. I realize that this means a lot to you, and I'm glad for your sake, really I am. Truth is, you even had me a bit worried about the kid. I'm sorry I was annoyed about being late to Marianne's party. Forgive me, sugar?"

"I'm the one who should say I'm sorry. It was my fault." Lorna knew he was turning on his charm, but she had never been able to resist it.

"Okay—we're both sorry." Farley laughed softly. "So how about changing your mind and going to Milli's tonight? You've done enough for one day."

"Oh, I wish I could . . . but this is my *job*." She was tempted to give in, because she could imagine all too clearly how Milli would behave, clinging to his arm, gazing up into his face, giving him her starry-eyed looks. But the answer was still no. "Will you go anyway?" she asked.

"It might be fun to drop by for a while. Nothing else to do." But Farley didn't sound depressed about it.

"Have a good time . . ." Lorna put the phone back. Would she and Farley ever reach an understanding? Or would it always be a case of having to "give in" to one another each time the question of her job came up? She sighed deeply.

It was almost eight-thirty when Lorna left the art class to attend the Y-teen meeting; and it was nine-thirty before that group broke up.

Just then Mary Renlo walked in, very enthusiastic about the success of her first art class. They sat by the fireplace, talking, until finally Bea glanced at her watch. "I must go home. Mother worries if I'm too late."

"Would you like to stop for a cup of coffee at The Pines?" Mary suggested as they prepared to leave.

Bea had to rush but Lorna replied, "I'd like to very much."

It was ten-thirty when they arrived at the restaurant. Since most of the tables were filled, they used the side entrance and took a small table near the door. Lorna had become fond of Mary in the few months she had known her, and they often talked quite freely to each other.

"I once considered becoming a social worker," Mary said, pensively stirring her coffee. "I get bored searching for things to keep me busy. I wish I had as much courage as Greg Taylor. He doesn't care what anyone thinks; he just does what he believes is right."

"You would have made a wonderful social worker," Lorna assured her. She wanted to ask about Gregory, but found it difficult to do so.

"I hope Marianne Blakely doesn't marry Greg," Mary said, frowning. "She wouldn't be good for him. Marianne's a cat." Suddenly her eyes widened in surprise. "Speak of the devil!" she said softly.

Lorna turned to see Marianne entering the front door with Jerry Lester, and behind them, Milli and Farley. "Let's leave," she whispered to Mary.

They paid their check at the table and slipped out through the side door. As they passed Farley's familiar car in the parking lot Lorna was almost in tears.

Mary must have noticed that her friend was upset for she said, "I guess they just dropped in for a late snack—probably a spur-of-the-moment idea."

"Probably," Lorna agreed, not mentioning that Milli had asked the crowd over to her house earlier that evening.

Mary gave her a smile and waved as she started her car. Lorna returned the wave, then hurried to the little Volkswagen. As she pulled out onto the street, the tears began to fall and she fumbled for a handkerchief and dried her eyes. The fresh night air cooled her cheeks and she rolled the car window down all the way, hoping her roommate would be asleep so she could go right to bed without talking.

Chapter Five

The next morning Lorna got up first and stole out of the apartment before her roommate woke up. Because she had slept poorly and her eyes felt heavy, she decided to walk to work, and felt better for it. All morning she busied herself with many tasks in an effort to put the Milli-and-Farley question out of her mind.

Shortly after eleven, her phone rang.

"Miss Evans? Greg Taylor, at the Child Guidance Clinic. Do you remember, we met the other night at Marianne's?"

"Of course I remember—didn't you rescue me?"

"You were doing all right without me!" His laugh was low and deep. "I'm calling about Judy Stillman. Dr. Marlow and I discussed the case yesterday, and I've just met her."

"I had no idea you would act so fast."

He laughed. "Well, this is more or less on my own. You see, Dr. Marlow is an old friend, and when he says a case is urgent, I know it is. He told me that you've also met Judy."

"I have. And I agree that it's urgent."

"I plan to give her some preliminary testing—but before I do, I want her to have a complete physical check-up. I made an appointment for her at the Pierce County Hospital, but she's too timid to go alone—" He hesitated. "I hate to ask, but since she has met you . . ."

"I'll be glad to take her. When is the appointment?"

"At two-thirty this afternoon."

"Does her father know?" Lorna asked.

"Yes; after talking with Dr. Marlow last night, he consented to the testing. That's a small step at least. As soon as I get the girl's medical report, I'd like to consult with you further."

"Any time." Lorna was pleased at the prospect of working with this quiet but forceful young man who cut through schedules for urgent cases. Not that all the children who came to the Clinic weren't in real need of help, but some situations were more critical than others. It was a great satisfaction to her to have Judy in such capable hands as Greg's.

She had scarcely hung up when the phone rang again. "Someone downstairs to see you, Miss Evans," Mrs. Whitney announced. She scooped up the letters that were ready to mail, and ran downstairs, wondering who her caller might be.

It was Farley! She caught a quick breath, then instinctively her hand went to her hair. She had a habit of running her fingers through her curls as she worked, and she had not taken even a peep in the mirror before leaving her office. She was suddenly conscious of the white blouse and tailored black skirt she was wearing. I must look great compared to the way Milli looked last night, she thought as he walked forward to meet her.

"I thought maybe you'd like to have lunch with me." This was the first time he had ever stopped in the Y during the day.

"Oh Farley, I'd love to . . ." She was just about to add, ". . . but I can't," when she caught herself. Hadn't she learned

• 55

anything from last night? "I'll go upstairs and get my coat," she said instead, noticing his quick smile of approval. In her office she glanced hurriedly into the mirror. Her hair wasn't as tousled as she had thought; it had a casual, wind-blown look, and she decided to leave it that way. She touched her lips with more color than usual, snatched up her suit jacket, gloves and pocketbook, and ran downstairs.

"Where to?" she asked as she and Farley settled themselves in the car.

"Wherever you say." She was so relieved to see him again that she felt indifferent to time—as long as she got back for Judy's two-thirty medical appointment.

"Larry's Dock?" This was a waterfront restaurant a few miles out of the city, featuring atmosphere as well as good food.

"Fine!"

She watched him out of the corner of her eye: as usual, he looked very handsome and it gave her an exciting feeling to be with him; everything they did was so much fun. Until last night, when she had seen him with Milli, she had not realized how she would feel if she were to lose him.

"Did you have a good time last night?" She had promised herself that she wouldn't ask any questions, but she had to know if their being together in the restaurant had any special significance.

"Oh sure. It was great." His expression told her nothing.

"Who was there?"

"Small party. Marianne, Herbie, Jerry, Dot—"

"Greg Taylor?" she asked.

"Old Greg doesn't go out much since he's come back." He chuckled. "Marianne's a bit put out about it."

"Is there anything serious between those two?"

"Serious with her, I'd say. And Marianne's a persistent

one. I wouldn't hold out much hope for Greg, if she makes up her mind—and I'd say she has."

"But they're so different!" Lorna heard herself protesting.

Farley smiled meaningly at Lorna. "Opposites attract, haven't you heard?" He always melted her with his smile and she felt her heart beat faster. "I've got a lot of faith in that old axiom, sugar. I think it applies to us."

"Perhaps it applies too much, Farley. I mean our backgrounds are so different——"

"Don't be silly!" He cut her off, his face serious now. "I'm crazy about you, sugar." The way he said it—"sugar"—sounded different this time: it was a caress.

"Milli's your type of girl." She had not meant to say that either; it was the wrong note, but he seemed to be avoiding any mention of The Pines.

"*You're* my kind, Lorna."

He must mean it or he wouldn't say it, she thought, but she wasn't very experienced at this sort of thing. Smooth remarks came all too readily in his crowd, she had observed.

"Once upon a time you probably said that to Milli!" She meant to sound light, gay, but it did not come out that way at all. It sounded as though she were hurt.

"What's got into you, honey?" He gave her a troubled frown and put his hand over hers. "Why all this harping on Milli?"

"You took her out after the party last night . . ." Maybe it was childish, silly, but she had to speak out and settle this thing. She wasn't good at pretending. He'd have to take her as she was—direct, honest—or not at all.

"How did you know that?" He began to laugh. "I didn't *take* her to The Pines, we all went together. I was home before midnight." Then he scowled. "Who told you anyway?"

"I saw you," she said in a small voice.

"Where were you? Why didn't you join us?"

"Mary Renlo and I just stopped by for a quick cup of coffee . . . we were in a hurry." That wasn't quite true, but she couldn't admit she had run away.

"Look, sugar, I like Milli. I've known her since we were kids; we were engaged for three months. But now you're my girl. Understand?" He gave her another look that melted her completely.

"I've been silly, Farley. I'm sorry . . ."

Suddenly he began to laugh and everything was all right. They reached Larry's Dock and he held her arm tightly as they walked into the dining room.

It was a leisurely, relaxed lunch. They gazed out the window, watching the bay rippling below; far out, there was only the blue horizon . . . the gulls and passing ships . . . At last Lorna had to look at her watch.

"It's nearly two o'clock. I've got to get back. Greg Taylor asked me to take a girl we're trying to help to a doctor," she told Farley.

"Greg Taylor!" He grinned at her. "I'm the one who should be jealous!"

"Don't be silly; this is business."

He held her chair as she stood up. "We must do this more often, sugar."

"A good way to get me fired!"

"You don't have to worry about that—they'd never find another gal to work all hours the way you do. However, if they *do* fire you, there's another job waiting for you. But the hours are longer, twenty-four of them, every day." Farley's eyes twinkled, but there was a serious undertone in his voice.

Lorna gave a little laugh and changed the subject, still not certain that she wanted to take his words as anything more than light-hearted banter.

She did not see Farley again until Friday. Since their luncheon date, her evenings had been filled with meetings: the Y Wives' Club, and a club for business girls on Wednesday; last night the Golden Age Club, a group whose members were all well over fifty. Tonight she and Farley were to have dinner at the Country House with Nola and Pete, and she was determined that nothing would interfere. As she covered her typewriter at the end of the day's work, however, the phone rang. Lorna made a face at it but picked it up dutifully.

Greg Taylor's pleasant voice answered her. "I have the reports on Judy Stillman, and I'd like very much to discuss them with you, Miss Evans."

"Of course. When?"

"Well, I have a meeting at six, but I thought I might run over to see you now if you're free."

"I'm free. As a matter of fact, I was just leaving. I have to go right past your office, why don't I stop in and save you the trip?"

"Fine, if you wouldn't mind. It's probably a better arrangement for both of us."

"I'll be there in a few minutes." Since he was giving his time to Judy's case, she certainly could do the same. As she drove along, she wondered what the results of Judy's tests had been . . .

On Wednesday, when she had reached the Stillman home to call for the girl, Judy did not come out. After blowing the car horn several times, Lorna finally had to get out and knock on the front door. There was still no answer, so she tried the handle and found the door unlatched. Judy was huddled in a chair in the dark hall, and only got up when Lorna smiled encouragingly at her. The girl spoke not a word until she reached the Volkswagen, then she gave a tiny smile. "It's like a toy car," she whispered.

On the trip downtown Judy asked questions about it, and seemed to be more at ease. As soon as they reached the hospital, however, she became apprehensive again. Fortunately, the doctor had a very gentle, friendly manner, and by the time she left his office, her fear had vanished completely. As they pulled up in front of the house, Lorna was surprised to see that Judy began to tremble.

"Are you afraid to go home?" Lorna asked. The girl shook her head, but shrank further down into the low seat.

"Sometimes I'm afraid," Lorna continued. "Everyone is."

"Are you afraid of people, or of the dark?"

"Of both sometimes."

"I'm afraid of people," Judy said.

"Any special people?"

The girl stared out the window silently.

Lorna had not pressed the question further, but since then the girl had been often in her thoughts . . .

Now Lorna found a parking space in front of the County City Building. When she reached the Child Guidance offices on the third floor, the receptionist admitted her into the private office at once. Smiling, Greg got up and offered her a chair. Behind his desk, he looked somehow older than he had at Marianne's. His dark hair lay close to his head, very thick and quite curly. As he picked up a sheaf of papers, Lorna noticed how long and sensitive his fingers were.

"Judy's medical report indicates that she is in generally good health; the I.Q. test results are surprisingly high." He studied one of the sheets. "However, she is very upset emotionally and needs immediate help."

"Dr. Marlow was right about getting her out of the home environment, of course, but what else would you suggest?" Lorna asked.

"Long-range counseling is the best solution. Our problem

is that she isn't eligible for help from the Welfare Department, because she is neither in need of financial assistance nor in trouble with the law. Only these emergencies are covered by welfare aid."

"That means she has to remain where she is! Is there *nothing* we can do?" Lorna could not conceal her distress.

"I think we can work something out. I talked with Grace Heaton earlier, over at Family Service, and that agency will handle Judy's counseling if we recommend it. They accept clients who can't pay any fee, but their schedule is so overcrowded that they can't possibly take her for several weeks." He leaned forward, his gray eyes on Lorna. "Meanwhile, I was wondering if you would take Judy into the Y, if there's an available room, and see what you can do with her."

"Oh we have the space, all right, but her father . . ."

"Mr. Stillman came here, at my request, this morning. He was really alarmed when I explained what the tests revealed. When he asked what he could do about the girl, I told him the only way to help her was to let her live at the Y and receive professional guidance for a while."

"What did he say to that?"

"Well, naturally, he tried to pooh-pooh the idea, saying all this guidance business was nonsense and what she needed was a firm hand. I got quite annoyed when he said that and told him bluntly that *his* firm hand hadn't been at all helpful to his daughter."

"From what I've heard about Mr. Stillman, I'm sure he didn't take that very well."

"No, he didn't. But he backed down a little and muttered something about who'd look after the house, he was getting old, etcetera. It was only when I said that Judy might end up in a hospital that he agreed to let her move into the Y—

on one condition: that she come home on week ends to help him with household chores and such."

"Did you accept his terms?"

"Under the circumstances, Miss Evans, I felt that it would defeat our purposes to refuse. If that's the only arrangement we can make at the moment, it's better than nothing. I'm convinced that he will eventually come around—but he's too stubborn to give in all the way now. It's almost certain that he will contribute to her support, but if he refuses, we'll manage."

Lorna had the definite feeling that, if necessary, Gregory Taylor intended to cover Judy's expenses himself, but she made no comment. She suspected that this quiet young man personally paid for a lot of things that fell outside the domain of welfare agencies.

"I'd like to see the girl settled as soon as possible. When could she move in, Miss Evans?"

"Mrs. Hart, our Housemother, said to bring her any time. All I have to do is give a few hours' advance notice, to be sure the room is made up."

"Fine! How about tomorrow?"

Lorna laughed. "You don't lose any time, do you? Tomorrow is perfectly all right. I'll inform Mrs. Hart in the morning, and drive out in the afternoon to pick Judy up. Shall I call Mr. Stillman, or will you?"

"I'll drop by the house this evening to see him. I can tell Judy to have her things ready by one o'clock tomorrow." He studied Lorna approvingly. "You believe in action too."

She felt herself blushing and to conceal her sudden embarrassment she asked, "Do you have any specific suggestions to make, as far as helping Judy is concerned?"

"I have a feeling that you know better than I what to do. She thinks you're wonderful." Greg smiled, as if he agreed with Judy. "But if you run into any difficulty, I'm as close as the telephone."

"I may have to take you up on that." They talked a few more minutes, then Lorna got up just as the secretary buzzed to announce the arrival of his next visitor.

When she left him, Lorna found herself even more impressed with Greg than before.

At home she found a note from Nola on the coffee table in the living room. Lorna threw herself down on the couch, kicked off her shoes, and read it:

See you two at the Country House—same time as planned. Peter had to stop at his office, so we left early. Don't be *too* late: we're both starving! Nola.

Lorna would have preferred to relax for a while, but her wristwatch told her that there was no time for such self-indulgence. Muttering to herself about always rushing somewhere, she picked up her pumps and padded into the bedroom in her stocking feet. A refreshing shower improved her mood and she hummed a tune as she put on her make-up and slipped into a black sheath dress—Farley's favorite. When the downstairs buzzer rang Lorna gave her hair one final pat, grabbed her coat, turned out the lights, and flew on winged feet down to the lobby, forgetting how tired she had felt a short half-hour ago.

It was a lovely evening as they drove along the water's edge, and half the stars seemed to have fallen into the bay. Farley slipped his arm around her. It was wonderful to be with him, to have him look down at her as if nothing mattered in all the world but she. They were now driving through the widely scattered suburban section, so there were fewer cars. It seemed to her that they were in a world alone, and she felt very close to him.

After parking near the tall pines surrounding the Country House, Farley took her in his arms.

"Nola and Pete are expecting us," she murmured, but held her face up for his kiss. His lips were cool against her own and she wished that they could somehow hold this moment forever . . .

When they entered the restaurant, the other couple was dancing. They made a striking pair: Peter, tall and broad-shouldered, handsome in a rugged way; Nola in her dark red dress, looking more like a model than a social worker.

"Good orchestra," Peter said, returning to the table as soon as Nola saw Lorna and Farley arrive.

"Have you two ordered yet?" Farley asked.

"Of course not—we were waiting for you." Nola slipped into the chair. "How about ordering first, then having a few dances while we wait? All in favor say Aye."

It was a unanimous decision and Farley turned to Lorna.

"Shall we dance, sugar?" He held her close and pressed his lips against her hair as they glided around the dance floor. The lights were low, the music was dreamy and soft: the setting could not have been more romantic.

"How long has it been since we've had an evening together?" Farley murmured. "It seems forever."

"Less than a week," she reminded him, but her voice was tender. His arm tightened around her and they said no more, giving themselves up to the spell of the music.

When the appetizers were served the two couples returned to the table. "We must do this more often," Peter said as they sat down.

"I agree—if I can ever persuade Lorna to take another

night off." Farley looked at Nola. "Tell me, do you work such long hours too?"

"I'm so crazy about my job, I never really think about the amount of time I put in," she replied candidly, and Lorna silently applauded her loyal friend. "But I don't work any harder than Pete—he's on call day and night for emergencies."

Peter grimaced. "Yeah, I'm lucky that way. But seriously," he continued after the others stopped laughing, "there's a lot more to this kind of work than meets the eye, Farley. Something's always coming up—kids running away, kids stealing cars, kids getting into bad accidents. Someone has to be around to take charge, help them out."

Farley began to show the usual restlessness that he displayed every time these serious discussions came up. "I know you're right, Pete; but it's three against one. Is there anything wrong with a fellow wanting to date his girl more than once a week—if he's lucky?"

"Of course there's nothing wrong with that," Nola spoke before the other two could say a word. "But you should dance at least *one* dance with the other girl in the party," and as Farley gallantly rose, bowed and held his arm out to Nola, she gave Lorna a broad wink.

"Leave it to her to pour oil on troubled waters," Peter said as he, too, rose and led Lorna to the floor. "And don't let Farley's talk bother you. Believe it or not, he boasts about you to his friends—how hard you work, how good you are at it."

"Really?" Lorna was genuinely surprised. "I wish he'd tell *me*."

Dinner was served as soon as they returned to the table. Peter kept them laughing throughout the meal, as if to erase the somber note that had been injected into the conversation earlier.

Watching Farley enjoying himself, Lorna suddenly thought, Life would be like this with him: gay, delightful. But she couldn't marry Farley—yet—she had just begun her work and she had promised to pay her parents back for sending her through school . . . Lorna caught herself up sharply. Why should she be thinking about marriage? Farley had not actually asked her to marry him, but he seemed to take it for granted that she would.

All those little remarks he made, the way he looked at her . . .

"Hey there, sugar, where are you?" Farley's voice broke through her thoughts, and Lorna quickly glanced over at Nola and Peter, who were grinning at her.

"Sorry," she said, "guess I was lost in thought."

"Lost is right," Peter told her. "We called your name twice and still you didn't hear."

Nola was slipping on her gloves. "We thought we'd take a short drive before going home. Okay with you?"

"I'm willing, if Farley is . . ." Lorna looked questioningly at him, and received a very definite nod of approval.

Farley turned the car onto the bridge that led to Halfway Point, overlooking the bay. Lorna, who had never been there at night, sighed happily as she gazed at the impressive view.

"We're up so high, I can see for *miles*. Oh, it's beautiful, with all those lights across the bay and on the water. I feel as if I'm standing somewhere up in heaven, looking down at the whole world . . ." She turned to Farley.

Little shivers began to race through her as he pulled her closer to him. "I'm crazy about you . . ." His lips found hers before she could reply; her arms went around his neck and she clung to him in a kiss that seemed to make the earth tremble. Never had she felt like this . . . she wanted him to hold her in his embrace forever.

Farley, too, was deeply stirred; his voice shook as he whispered against her cheek: "Lorna sweet, we've got to talk about us. I want you to marry me soon, very soon——"

At that moment the lights of a car cut a double path through the darkness and Pete's voice reached their ears: "Okay, kids, break it up now."

"Stop acting like a policeman—even if you are one," Farley told him gruffly, only half kidding.

But Lorna felt strangely grateful for the interruption. What was the matter with her? A week ago she had been terrified that he would go back to Milli. Now, when he was proposing, she didn't want to hear him say the words . . . she didn't want to have to give an answer . . .

When the other couple got out of their car to stand at the railing overlooking the bluff, she said, coaxingly, "Let's get out too." Farley unwillingly consented and they joined Nola and Pete.

After a few minutes Nola turned to get back in the car. "Much as I hate to end this moonlight vigil," she announced, "we'd better leave. I have a nine o'clock appointment tomorrow morning."

"I have a few things to take care of at the Y myself," Lorna added. "We'll be leaving too." Without knowing why, she did not want to remain at Halfway Point with Farley; and he did not press her to stay.

"I'll follow your car," Peter called out just before he slammed his door.

"Police escort, eh?" Farley called back, starting the engine.

Neither of them spoke on the way home, but when they reached the apartment building, Farley put his hand out to hold her back. "We haven't finished our conversation, sugar."

"It's late, darling, and I really am tired," she parried.

"Okay . . . but I won't let you put me off longer than

tomorrow. How about going out in the boat in the afternoon —say around three?"

"Just the two of us?"

"Yes, I want to be alone with you for a change. We can discuss—things; make plans . . ." His kiss was tender, lingering, and Lorna's heart was pounding again.

She drew away gently, smiling at him in the half-darkness. "I can't *think* straight when you do that, much less make plans. Besides, Nola's waiting for me. Thank you for a heavenly evening, Farley . . . Call me tomorrow around noon. Good night." And she slipped out of the car before he could stop her.

Chapter Six

The first thing Lorna saw on her desk when she arrived at the Y on Saturday morning was an envelope postmarked Grand Mound. Without even waiting to take off her coat she tore it open, scarcely noticing the five-dollar bill that fell out as she unfolded the letter. Quickly she read through the scrawled note:

Dear Miss Evans,

I am sure glad I have you to write to. We are allowed to write to two relatives and one friend, and you're the only friend I have.

I'm trying very hard to be good, like you said, so the year will go by quickly and I'll be free. I keep thinking about studying hard and learning something so I can get a job when I get out. You said I could make something of myself and I'm going to.

Do you still mean it, about me coming back to the Y.W.C.A. when I'm out? I've got to know for sure and have it to look forward to, or maybe I can't keep on trying. I'm sending back the money you loaned me. I guess I have a lot to be grateful for—if it wasn't for you I just don't know what would have happened to me. Thank you, Miss Evans, I sure hope you write me sometime soon.

Seriously yours,
Glennie Ross

Tears came to Lynn's eyes and she hoped with all her heart that the year would pass quickly for little Glennie. On a sudden impulse she turned to her typewriter and typed a long, friendly reply before settling down to answer several business letters that had also arrived.

Afterward, she checked with Mrs. Hart, and was assured that Judy's room was ready and waiting.

It was a few minutes before one when Lorna arrived at the Stillman home. Reverend Marlow had phoned earlier to say that Judy's father would not let the girl leave until the housework was done. Mr. Stillman was nowhere in sight, much to Lorna's relief. The front door was half open, and she walked in when her knock was not answered. Seeing no one in the living room, she wandered toward the rear of the house and finally found Judy standing in the kitchen staring out the window. A stack of dishes filled the sink.

"Hello, Judy, need any help?" Lorna asked quietly.

The girl started. "Oh! Miss Evans, you came . . . No, I can do these myself."

"Two can do them faster," Lorna replied, pushing up her sleeves.

"Are your things packed?" she asked when they had finished in the kitchen. Judy led her into her bedroom and pointed to a suitcase on the bed.

"Yes, but I don't see how I can go."

"Why not?" Lorna lifted the suitcase.

Judy's hands fluttered nervously. "There's all this work. I'm so slow, I never get things done."

"But your father knows you're going, my dear."

"Oh, yes, I guess he does . . . Well then . . ."

"Do you know where he is?" Lorna asked, and when she got a negative head shake in reply, she guided Judy firmly out of the house and into the car.

On the way to the Y, she began to explain what the Residence was like, but the girl scarcely listened to a word. Mrs. Hart's warm welcome, however, banished some of Judy's fear and she showed a slight interest when she saw the large kitchen, where the girls could cook, and the cheerful room she was to have. Her eyes lingered on the pretty rose-printed drapes and matching bedspread. "Pink is my favorite color," she whispered, glancing shyly at the Housemother.

Mrs. Hart took Judy to her apartment, and when Lorna joined them there later, she found them brewing a pot of tea.

She stopped long enough to have a cup with them, then said she had to be leaving.

"I think it's best to have Judy eat with me," Mrs. Hart explained at the door, "until she feels more at home." Lorna went home feeling that things were going well, for the moment at least.

Nola, looking chic as well as comfortable in capri pants, was pouring herself some coffee when Lorna walked into the apartment.

"Hi! That's what I call perfect timing. I just made a fresh pot." When Lorna refused, Nola asked, "What's the matter, pet? Was it pretty rough?"

"Oh, you know how I am. I get too involved in these cases. But that Stillman girl is so defenseless." She dumped her coat on one end of the couch, wriggled her feet out of her shoes, and flopped down at the other end. "I wonder how long you have to be in this business to become completely objective."

"One never does, I suspect. Today, for instance, I interviewed a couple who want to adopt a baby. We can't grant their request because they're over the age limit and he isn't well. But I found myself wanting to bend the rules for them." Nola stared reflectively into space. "But the child is our first concern, and we must be realistic. We can't change facts and we can't take obvious risks."

"When you were in school, Nola, did you ever think some of the cases you'd have would be so tragic?"

"Well, not exactly. A lot of things were purely theoretical, as far as I was concerned. Even though we were warned, we were too young, inexperienced, and idealistic for the warning to sink in." Nola smiled wryly. "When they said we'd have to achieve emotional maturity, they meant it, pet."

"And patience. As Mae Devlin says, we often don't see results quickly. Greg Taylor cautioned me in Judy's case that it will take time . . ."

"Where did you see Greg?" Nola raised an inquisitive eyebrow.

"I dropped by his office after work yesterday to discuss the case with him."

"He's very nice, and wonderful to work with," Nola said. "We've referred some of our troubled children to him." Nola's work with the Child Welfare Division brought her into contact with disturbed children as well as orphans and those who needed foster homes. "You know, I've often wondered what happened to kids before social work was introduced into this country. State welfare work wasn't really organized until after the depression. Do you realize that this year over four hundred thousand children are receiving welfare services? In addition, think of all the assistance to families and to our senior citizens. The way the field is growing, it's no wonder they need twenty thousand trained people to fill the vacancies this year!"

"I wonder if Mary Richmond ever dreamed, years ago when she started case work, that it would grow the way it has? According to the latest statistics, we have one hundred thousand workers in the United States."

"And don't forget Jane Addams. Think of what she started with that first settlement house!" Nola added, smiling.

"You know, it's odd but the fields of social work are not as clear-cut as they were a few years ago, when we began our professional training. Students still major in the five fields— psychiatric work, group work, community organization, medical work, research—but they are overlapping more and more. The new theory is that a social worker can function in any of the fields if she has a broad basic training." Recently Lorna had been giving considerable thought to the matter, now that she had taken over Mae's counseling at the Y. "As a matter of fact, I've been considering the idea of doing case work entirely."

"I'm not surprised, and I think you'd be excellent at it, really I do. But that's a decision you'd better reserve for later." Nola glanced meaningly at the clock. "Isn't Farley almost due?"

Lorna took one look at her watch and dashed into the bedroom as Nola picked up the coffee tray and carried it to the kitchenette. "I'm going down to the laundry," she called out. "You can make your own excuses this time."

"I'll be ready for him, wait and see!"

Driving down the winding road along the bay to the Yacht Club, Lorna was amazed at the number of boats docked at the piers. The day was perfect, blending the crisp freshness of the air with the salt-water tang of the sea.

Out on a pier, Farley stopped alongside one of the boats. "This is the Comet," he announced, not trying to conceal his pride.

"She's larger than I expected!" Lorna exclaimed. "But she's as graceful as a swan!"

"That may be, but she's a lot faster," he replied laughing.

She was surprised at the roominess, the luxury of the boat. An elderly man on deck tipped his hat as they came aboard and Farley introduced him as Jim Morgan. "Old Jim," as Farley fondly called him, kept the Comet spotless and shining, and now, having prepared food in the small galley, was about to go ashore.

Leading Lorna forward to the wheelhouse, Farley picked up a captain's hat and put it on with a self-conscious grin. "Custom," he explained briefly.

The cruiser edged away from the pier and headed for open water, with Lorna standing beside Farley at the wheel. She threw back her head and let the breeze whip her short hair, gazing ahead at the vast stretch of gray-blue water, dotted with green islands. She smiled up at Farley, her breath catching a little with the excitement of it, and he put an arm around her.

He pointed to an island they were approaching. "We'll anchor off-shore there and have dinner," he said.

With the sun slowly sliding into the sea behind the small green jewel of land, he could not have chosen a lovelier spot. Lorna wanted to go over to the sandy beach but he told her that it would be dark too soon. "We'll come back another time and spend the whole day there," he promised. He led her into the galley, exchanging his captain's cap for a high white chef's cap. He would not let Lorna help with the food, but allowed her to set the table. The window above it gave them a full view of the wooded island and they could hear the music of the wild birds.

Dinner over, they went out on deck and leaned against the railing that separated them from the darkening water. The sun was a diminishing blaze of orange that disappeared even as they watched. Farley's arm encircled Lorna, and it seemed as if the magic of the sunset had cast a spell over the sea, the boat, the two people on it . . . "It's wonderful," she said softly. "I used to be afraid of the water. I'm not any more—not now."

"That's because I'm with you." He looked down at her. "You're beautiful, Lorna." He touched her hair, then suddenly she was in his arms. "I love you, darling." His voice was low, husky. "I want to marry you." She pressed her face against the soft wool of his sweater. Last night she had not wanted him to speak of love, but now his words seemed as natural as the sunset. He raised her face. "You love me, don't you, darling?" His lips were close to hers, his arms strong and wonderful, his eyes full of tenderness.

"I love you, Farley," she wispered.

When they started back, Lorna gazed thoughtfully out over the now black water as Farley stood at the wheel. He called her to join him, and she walked slowly to his side.

"Have you ever stopped to consider how different we are?" she asked.

"When you love someone, what do differences matter?" His answer seemed reasonable enough now, in the quiet evening, with the magic still upon them—but how would it seem tomorrow? Lorna did not know.

"There's so much we have to learn about each other," she persisted. "After all, marriage is one of the most important

• 75

steps in life. You haven't met my parents; I don't know yours——"

"We'll correct that. Mother wants you to come to dinner tomorrow evening. She wants very much to meet you; in fact she suggested it herself several times. She's pretty sharp, you know. I guess she has it figured out already. Anyway, she'll call you tomorrow."

"I'll be delighted to come," Lorna replied quietly, hoping that she was concealing her nervousness at the prospect of meeting her future in-laws.

By six o'clock the next day Lorna was roaming the living room, too restless to sit and wait for Farley. Last night she had come home, eager to tell Nola the news of Farley's proposal, only to find a note saying that Nola and Peter had gone to visit Peter's sister and her husband and would return Sunday evening. Lorna had kept busy most of the day, going to church in the morning, stopping at the Y to see Judy, coming home to wash her hair and do her nails and she still had plenty of time to dress for dinner at the Knowleses'. But no matter what she did, she could not escape the fact that she was worried about meeting Farley's family.

The silence in the apartment was finally too much for her, and she picked up her coat and went down to the lobby to wait. Just as she got there, Farley walked up the front steps. Without a word, he put his arms around her for a brief moment and some of her anxiety vanished. The way he held her, the way he looked down at her, reassured her.

As soon as they got into the car, he held out a small velvet box. Opening it, he took out the most beautiful diamond ring she had ever seen.

"Oh Farley!" she cried. "It's—it's gorgeous! But I can't wear it—we haven't really made any plans . . . there's so much to decide——" He slipped the ring on the third finger of her left hand, and his lips found hers, silencing her protests.

"You like it?" he whispered, kissing her again before she could answer. "Never mind about plans, decisions, arrangements. You're going to marry me—everything else will take care of itself." He smiled down at her. "You are beautiful, darling, and I love you very much."

He started the car while Lorna gazed at the sparkling diamond ring, at the pale gold moon climbing into the sky, at the stars, which had taken on a special brilliance.

As they neared his house, Farley turned to her. "When *are* you going to marry me? They'll ask, you know."

She looked at him, startled. "I really don't know . . . In the spring, next year perhaps. After all, this only happened last night!"

"You must have known I was going to propose, sugar. A girl can tell."

"Well . . . I couldn't." That was not quite true but she didn't want to admit that he was right. "Please don't rush me, Farley; there are so many things to consider——"

"Like what? I love you, you love me, what else is there?"

"My work, my family." She put her hand on his arm imploringly. "Please, darling, must we decide this minute?"

He hesitated a moment, then replied, "Whatever you want, sugar."

The Knowles house was hidden behind a high hedge in a cluster of pines; below it lay a lake. It was a large house, where three generations of Knowles had lived, and tonight all the lights were on, the crystal chandeliers shining through the windows like clusters of brilliant stars.

Farley's mother met them at the door. She was a tall, dark woman with patrician features. "We are very happy to meet you at last, my dear," Mrs. Knowles said, extending her hand. "Farley has told us what a lovely girl you are."

Mr. Knowles joined the group as they walked into the living room. "He has indeed!" he said emphatically.

"I think it's so nice that your home is in Seattle, so close for the wedding," Mrs. Knowles said, over coffee and dessert. "You will have a big wedding, won't you, my dear? You see, with no daughter of my own, I can only look forward to my son's wedding."

"Well, of course I haven't had time to think about any kind of a wedding yet," Lorna stammered. "It takes time and—and my mother and father are in California for the winter . . ." She broke off, aware that her words made it sound like a winter holiday for her parents. All evening she had been painfully conscious of the luxurious furnishings of the Knowles home, the evidence of wealth all about her. What would Mrs. Knowles think of the shabby comfort of their Seattle house, their frugal way of life?

"Will you write them the news or call them?" Mrs. Knowles was asking. "They will be thrilled, naturally."

As they settled themselves around the living room fireplace, Lorna found herself worrying about a large wedding on her small budget. How could she tell them it was out of the question, and that her family could not afford it?

When asked about her job at the Y.W.C.A., Lorna tried to explain the great need for social work in the community, while Mrs. Knowles listened politely.

"Yes, of course, dear, but naturally you won't continue to work after you're married." Farley's mother was not asking a question, she was making a statement.

"Well, I hadn't actually intended——" Before Lorna could finish the sentence with the words, *to stop working*," the older woman continued:

"That's what I thought. You can always volunteer an hour or two a week at one of the hospitals, if you want to continue your social work."

Oh dear, thought Lorna, she wasn't listening at all when I was explaining just now. They'll never understand me—nor I them.

Farley said, "Don't worry, Mother, Lorna and I will arrange something satisfactory."

Mrs. Knowles looked vaguely unhappy about the whole thing.

After a few moments of awkward silence, Mrs. Knowles looked at Lorna. "Do you play bridge, my dear?"

"No, I'm sorry I don't," Lorna said regretfully. "I never had a chance to learn."

"Oh, that's unfortunate, but never mind—you can take lessons. It's such a pleasant game for a foursome. Milli and Farley used to play with us often——" She paused and glanced quickly at her guest. "I'm sorry, that was tactless of me . . ."

"Not at all, Mrs. Knowles. Why shouldn't you mention Milli's name? I knew she was once engaged to Farley." Lorna held her head high, her eyes steady on the other woman.

"That's right, Mother. I have no secrets from Lorna," Farley added, somewhat belatedly, Lorna thought.

Mr. Knowles finally steered the conversation into safer waters, and two hours passed pleasantly before Lorna glanced at her watch and said it was time to leave. Farley's mother rose smoothly.

"You must come again soon, very soon. Perhaps for lunch one day, while the men are not around? We must get acquainted and it's always easier without them." With a smile she took Lorna's arm and led her out into the hall, where Farley was getting their coats. Mr. Knowles stood quietly while the two women finished their good-byes.

"Do call about lunch this week, my dear."

Lorna promised she would and turned to shake hands with Mr. Knowles. He looked directly into her blue eyes and, as if he liked what he saw, he nodded firmly. "Yes, young lady, I think you'll make my son an excellent wife—bridge or no bridge." He winked and patted her shoulder lightly.

In the car, Farley said, "Look, sugar, I know it was a bit of an ordeal, meeting the family, but the first time is the hardest. Mom and Dad are really very sweet people."

"Mmmm," she agreed sleepily.

At the apartment door she put her arms around his neck. "Good night, dear," she whispered, kissing the tip of his ear.

He held her tightly, reluctant to let her go. "Let's make it soon, sugar—the wedding." He kissed her once, twice, lightly. "I'm a very impatient guy!"

Lorna unlocked the door. "So I've heard," she said, making a face at him over her shoulder as she went in.

"See you tomorrow," he called softly through the door, and then she heard his rapid footsteps on the stairs.

She walked slowly into the bedroom, turned on the dressing-table lamp and studied the reflection of the diamond ring in the mirror as she moved her hand about to catch the light on the beautiful gem. She wished Nola were back, so she could tell her the news . . .

Without bothering to slip off her dress, she stretched out on her bed and thought about Mrs. Knowles and her own mother, wedding invitations and honeymoon trips. One notion after another came to her, and she was deep in reverie when Nola appeared in the bedroom doorway.

"Hi! You're home earlier than usual, aren't you, pet? Everything okay?"

Lorna sat up, smoothing her hair. "Everything's fine."

"In that case, come on out and have some hot chocolate

with Pete and me. He's making it because he says mine tastes like dishwater."

"I heard that," Peter's voice boomed out from the next room, "and I *did not* say that—even though it's true."

Both girls laughed, then Nola said, "Never mind looking around for your shoes—this is a come-as-you-are party."

Lorna obediently padded along behind her friend and curled up in her favorite corner of the living room couch.

As Pete handed her a cup of chocolate, he let out a long, low whistle. "Where did you get that rock?" He put down the other cup he was holding, and motioned Nola to his side.

"Come now, young lady, confess! Is this what I think it is?" he asked.

"Of course it is, silly," Nola replied, reaching out for Lorna's hand. "Oh, it's beautiful! Why didn't you say something about this? We should be drinking champagne instead of cocoa—except that's all we have. Congratulations, pet; I'm so happy for you."

"Stop monopolizing the bride-to-be and give somebody else a chance," Peter ordered, and bent down to kiss Lorna. "Farley's a lucky fellow—I always said so. You two really have it made." He raised his cup high, declaiming, "Here's to the future Mrs. Farley Knowles!" After Nola repeated the gesture and the toast, the two of them solemnly sipped their cocoa, making big eyes at Lorna over the rim of their cups.

"Cut it out, you two clowns, you're embarrassing me!" Lorna laughed. "It's only an engagement, after all."

"*Only!*" Pete and Nola said simultaneously, and they all settled down to their cocoa and conversation. Finally the handsome young police lieutenant looked at the clock on the desk and got up.

"I've got a big day tomorrow so any further details of this momentous occasion will have to wait." Nola walked him to the door. "Don't you two stay up half the night talking. You're working girls, you know."

Nola could hardly wait to hear more about Lorna's first visit to the Knowleses' home. "Did he give you the ring there?" she wanted to know.

As they got ready for bed Lorna told her about Farley's proposal and the meeting with his family.

"He wants us to be married soon, but I don't know . . . there are so many things to discuss, to plan . . . We are so different . . ."

"I know, pet," Nola said gently. "Pete and I are different too. But I'd marry him the minute he asked me. If you love a guy, what do you want to wait for?"

"It sounds silly, I suppose, but I just can't rush into this thing. It's all happened too suddenly for me. I need more time."

"You know best, Lorna. Each gal has to decide for herself. But Farley won't wait long—he's not the kind."

"That's what he said on the way home," Lorna murmured thoughtfully as she climbed into bed.

Chapter Seven

The two weeks following Lorna's engagement were wonderfully happy ones. Even the rainy season, which had come in earnest, could not dim the excitement. Several parties were given for them, and that first Saturday Farley asked Nola and Peter to join them on the Comet for an all-day picnic outing. In return, Pete got four tickets for a play at the Little Theater the following Friday night.

Lorna wrote to her folks, telling them the news, though she did not mention Farley's wealth. She did describe, however, the dinner at his home and casually mentioned the boat. In their reply neither of her parents referred to these items. *I'm glad you're happy, Lorna girl*, her father wrote. *This Farley Knowles had better be a fine man!*

What about your work? her mother inquired. *Will you be giving it up when you marry?* This question was the one problem that troubled Lorna, for she could not persuade Farley to discuss it. Each time she tried, he passed it off lightly, evading a direct answer. "Time enough to decide that when you set the wedding date, sugar," he would say. Or, "I'm not planning to put you in prison, darling, I'm only planning to marry you." But she had an uneasy feeling that he felt the same way his mother did about the matter.

She would miss her work if she had to give it up, Lorna thought as she cleared her desk that Friday night. Everything at the Y had been going exceptionally well with the groups she had already organized; and her latest idea, a class for the "solo" parent, was more successful than she had hoped for. This group of parents, who were raising children without the help of a mate, welcomed the opportunity to discuss problems and exchange ideas, and Grace Heaton, head of the Family Service Agency in Tacoma, found great satisfaction in conducting the class. One evening after she had finished, Grace had dropped by Lorna's office for a chat. During the course of their conversation the subject of counseling came up.

"You seem to have a real feeling for it," Grace had said with her usual candor, "which isn't always true with beginning workers."

"I was raised with people's problems," Lorna had replied, thinking of the countless hours she had spent with her mother visiting families in distress.

"If you ever decide to go into full-time counseling, let me know," Grace said. "Not that I plan to steal a first-class group worker from Mae Devlin. If she knew I even breathed such an idea, she'd have my scalp." She laughed in her frank and charming way. Grace and Mae were the best of friends.

If she were not planning to marry, Lorna thought as she put on her coat and left her office, she might consider counseling as a field, but with marriage even a year away, it would be foolish to change, especially since she was happy at the Y.

As she entered the Residence section, she heard voices nearby. Down the hall three girls were whispering together at the door of the Rest Room, and they ran toward her when they saw her.

"Oh Miss Evans," Betty Morton cried excitedly, "Judy Stillman's in the washroom and won't come out."

"She's been in there almost an hour, just standing and staring at the wall. She won't even talk to us!" Sally Williams' blue eyes were as round as her face. "Is she crazy or something?"

"She's probably ill," Lorna replied, hoping that her alarm was not apparent to the three girls.

"I don't think so. I asked her," Lenore Coleman, the oldest one, answered. "She doesn't say anything, just stares at the wall."

"It gives me the creeps." Sally shuddered. "Do you think she might be crazy, Miss Evans?"

"Of course she isn't," Lorna said firmly, wondering exactly what to tell them. They could be very helpful in this situation, if she didn't say the wrong thing and frighten them. "Judy is afraid," she began cautiously, "so much so that she can scarcely talk to people. Unless we help her, she may never be able to make friends, have dates, or take a job, or do any of the things you girls do."

"Really?" Sally gasped. "How awful!" Sally had never been scared of anyone in her life. She was a thorough little extrovert.

Betty looked incredulous. "We thought she just didn't like us!"

"What can we do to help?" Lenore asked. "We'd all be glad to, if we only knew how."

"First of all, don't rush her." Lorna smiled at them. "These things take time. Judy has never been away from home before, but gradually she'll be more at ease here. Meanwhile, just be patient and friendly with her. You'll find ways to help her as time goes on, I'm sure." Lorna sounded a lot more confident than she felt. "Now I'd better go in and talk to her. Perhaps it would make it easier for her if you didn't mention this little episode to any of the other girls."

"We won't say a word, Miss Evans." The girls walked away slowly, looking back at her worriedly.

Lorna went over to the Rest Room and, after listening for a second outside, opened the door. "Judy . . . Judy . . ."

There was no answer.

The room seemed to be empty. There was no one in any of the compartments. Walking around the last compartment, she found Judy standing with her face to the wall. She did not turn as Lorna approached, but she hunched her thin shoulders as if to protect herself.

"Judy." Lorna spoke gently.

A quiver went through the small form, but there was no answer.

"Judy." She put some authority into her voice this time, and the girl half turned, her face as white as the wall. "What are you afraid of, Judy? Let me help you, dear."

"I don't want to be afraid." The voice was scarcely a whisper. "I've tried not to be afraid."

"I thought you were getting along so well, and you told me you liked it here—remember?" Lorna took the thin hands in her own. "Has something happened?"

"He calls me. Every night he calls me. And I have to go home again today."

"You don't want to go?"

"When I think of it, I—I want to hide so no one will ever find me."

"Would you like me to talk with your father? Suppose I ask him to let you stay here this week end, every week end, until you are ready to visit him?"

"He would think I asked you to do it." Judy shivered.

"Is he coming to pick you up?"

"Yes . . . he'll be here in a few minutes."

"I'll talk to him, dear. You just go back to your room and I'll tell him you're staying here."

"No! No, no!" There was panic in Judy's voice.

"Can't you trust me, Judy?"

The phone in the hall rang. One of the girls answered it and called loudly, "Judy, Judy Stillman, your dad's in the lobby."

Judy trembled so violently that Lorna became alarmed.

"I'm going down to speak with him. But first I'll walk you to your room, and I don't want you to come down under any circumstances. Will you do that, Judy?"

"Yes, Miss Evans."

Lorna led her down the hall and opened her room door. "I'll be back in a few minutes; just wait here for me."

When she left, Judy was sitting very straight on the chair. Her big eyes were dry, staring straight ahead. "I've *got* to persuade him to leave her here," Lorna said to herself. "I don't know what will happen if I fail."

Judy's father was in the library, pacing back and forth like a caged bear. He looked a little like a bear, too, Lorna thought, with his dark, shaggy hair that needed cutting.

Mr. Stillman, who had his back to the door, must have thought she was Judy, for he whirled about. "You know I don't like to be kept waiting!" When he saw it wasn't his daughter, he frowned angrily, his eyes almost disappearing under his shaggy brows.

"I'm Lorna Evans." In spite of her firm resolve, she was intimidated by this gruff man.

"You're the one who brought Judy here." He regarded her with belligerence.

"Your daughter isn't feeling well tonight, Mr. Stillman. I wonder if you'd mind if she stayed here this week end?"

"Of course I'd mind. Who's gonna catch up on the work at home?"

No wonder Judy was afraid of him; Lorna was so nervous that she had to lean against a chair for support. "Judy isn't well," she said again. "She wouldn't be able to work if she came home." She drew a deep breath. "I'm going to talk to you plainly, Mr. Stillman. Judy gets upset every time she goes home. Her visits must stop until she is better . . ."

"Look here, young lady, I agreed to let her come on condition she come back home week ends. You folks ain't got the say of her."

"I've discussed Judy's case with the doctor," Lorna told him, "and unless she can be brought out of this state of anxiety and fear, she will have a complete breakdown. If that happens, she'll be of no help to you or anyone else. You might even have to pay for her in an institution for the rest of her life." Her words had a surprising effect on him, and she followed it up. "If you will just leave her here, I'm sure we can help her. She'll receive training so that she can get a job and support herself. Wouldn't *that* be better for both of you?"

He thought it over, glaring at her out of those fierce black eyes. "The kid'll be eighteen in six months anyway, an' I suppose I couldn't keep her home then if she took a notion to leave. But I'm warnin' you—if my daughter gets into any trouble, I'll have the law on you!" He continued to glare for a moment, then swung around and stalked out.

Lorna's knees felt as if they would no longer support her, and she eased herself into the chair. She had won a reprieve for Judy!

She hurried from the library and dashed up the stairs.

Judy was still sitting in the chair, but she had a book on her lap now.

"Your father has gone, Judy." Lorna sat down on the bed near her. "You don't have to go home until you want to." Judy did not move or speak and Lorna had a moment of fear. Had this come too late? Had she failed with Judy, now that she had made this bargain with the father? She searched for the right words. "Will you let us help you, dear? We all want to help you—Mrs. Hart, Miss Devlin, me . . ."

Judy looked at Lorna trustingly. "I'll do whatever you say, Miss Evans."

Lorna could not recall ever having been so touched. Impulsively she wanted to put her arms about Judy, but knew that she must not. "I don't know if I am wise enough to know what is best always, but I care very much what happens to you and I'll try to advise you the right way. Mrs. Hart will help too. You like Mrs. Hart, don't you?"

"Oh, very much."

"We must plan for your future also. What would you like to be, if you had your choice of anything in the world?"

"I'd like to be a nurse's aid. More than anything, I'd like to help people who are sick."

"That's a very worth-while thing to do, and I know you'd be wonderful at it. We must see if we can arrange it." Lorna made a mental note to talk to Greg Taylor about it. She had great confidence in him.

"Everyone here likes you, Judy. The girls want to be your friends if you will let them."

"They do?" A smile caught at Judy's lips. "It would be nice to have friends. I used to . . ." Her voice sounded dreamy.

"I'm going down to Mrs. Hart's apartment now. Why don't you lie down for a while? Mrs. Hart will call you at dinner-time."

"All right." Obediently Judy got up from her chair as

• 89

Lorna walked to the door. She smiled reassuringly at the girl and received the shadow of a smile in return. In the House-keeper's quarters, Lorna recounted the happenings of the past hour.

"Now we can really begin to help her," Mrs. Hart sighed. "But I doubt that she's ready for schooling yet. If only she'd mix with the girls more."

"We'll think of a way to get her started." Lorna rose to go. "Until she's ready for school, we'd better continue the sewing you got her interested in. She does beautiful work."

"She's learning to cook new dishes too. I enjoy having her here."

"You do wonders for these girls. We would be lost without you," Lorna said sincerely. She left then, feeling that Judy was in good hands. Mrs. Hart was right, of course; Judy could not function in school until she could mingle more freely with people.

Lorna kept turning the question over in her mind that evening as she dressed for the theater. Nola was late getting home. "I thought I'd never make it," she said, coming in, breathless. "Mr. Friederickson, the father of one of my fam-ilies, called to say that his wife had a sudden gall-bladder attack and had to be rushed to the hospital. He was frantic. There are six children at home, all under ten. I calmed him down, then had to find someone to stay with the youngsters." As she talked, she was changing her clothes. "What exciting things happened to you today?"

Lorna told her about Judy as they fixed a quick snack and Nola nodded approvingly when she heard the outcome of Mr. Stillman's visit to the Y. Miraculously, the two girls were ready when Peter and Farley arrived.

It was toward the end of the second act that Lorna sud-denly thought of a way to help Judy. The Residence girls were planning to give a play in November to raise money for a television set, and there was a part in it for a pianist. If they could get Judy to participate in the play, it would serve to bring her into close contact with the other girls, and also give her more self-confidence.

During the next intermission Lorna mentioned her idea to Nola.

"And who is this Judy?" Farley wanted to know.

"One of the girls at the Y. Oh Farley, I've been racking my brains for a way to help her overcome her fear of people."

"She's scared to death, and you're going to put her in a play! That sounds a bit silly, doesn't it?" Farley shook his head in wonder.

"Not at all. In acting, you forget your real self as you act out another role. Psychologists use a similar technique with children in order to observe their behavior and learn their problems, which they are too young to understand and express in their own words."

"That's right, they do," Peter agreed.

"But would Judy do it?" Nola wondered.

"She might, if I coax her," Lorna answered. "She seems to trust me. It's worth a try anyhow, isn't it?"

"I'll bet you've been thinking about that all during this play!" Farley handed her a paper cup of iced orange juice from the refreshment bar. "I'll bet you don't even know what's happening onstage."

"Of course I do. Now who's being silly?"

"I agree with you, Lorna—it's worth a try," Nola decided.

Farley groaned. "Okay, girls, break it up."

"All right." Lorna laughed. "I won't mention it again."

"I thought I saw my old friend Greg Taylor down front," Farley said. "Let's try to locate him."

Peter nodded toward the doorway. "Isn't that Greg over there?"

"You're right; he's with Marianne," Farley said, pleased. He caught Greg's eye and raised his hand. "Let's ask them to stop at the New Yorker with us after the show. Okay, Pete?"

"It's fine by me."

As the buzzer sounded for the third act, Greg and Marianne came toward them. Farley murmured something to Greg and received a nod, but there was no time for proper greetings. The house lights dimmed just as they reached their seats.

The three couples met again when the play was over. Marianne was looking very elegant in a red silk dress, with her hair in a new upswept style. Lorna had seen her only once since the party for Milli. At a large round table in the New Yorker, Lorna was seated between Farley and Greg; Marianne, who was sitting next to Peter, seemed captivated by him. She had never met him before, and was asking all sorts of questions about his work. Nola was chatting with Farley, so Lorna turned to Greg. "I had a show-down with Mr. Stillman tonight," she said. "He has promised to leave Judy alone."

"He has!" Greg whistled softly. "Tell me more."

Lorna was in the midst of her story when suddenly there was a lull at the table and her words came out clearly in the silence. "I don't know whether what I did was right or not—" She caught herself and looked around laughing.

"What are you two so engrossed in?" Marianne asked curiously.

"Oh, it's business, really," Lorna replied.

"Not again!" Farley raised his hands helplessly.

She made a face at him. "I didn't think you'd hear."

"Tell it so we can all enjoy it." Marianne leaned forward, smiling.

"I'm sorry," Lorna said, feeling embarrassed now. "It's confidential."

"Oh come on, we're all friends." Marianne turned her face saucily to Greg. "Tell her she can let us in on it too, Greg honey."

"She really can't, you know," he shook his head.

Marianne tossed her head. "Oh you and your silly secrets."

Lorna gave her an annoyed glance, which Farley must have noticed, for he pushed back his chair. "Hey, we're out for a social evening, not a social workers' convention. Let's dance." He smiled in his charming way, and Lorna was thankful for that.

"Great idea." Peter got up and held Nola's chair. Greg and Marianne followed them onto the floor.

"Can't you leave your problems at the Y?" Farley asked when they could not be heard by the others. "I've got business problems, but I don't bring them to parties with me."

"You're right," Lorna agreed contritely. "I really shouldn't talk about them. You were sweet to get me out of that awkward spot with Marianne."

"Marianne can be a little difficult at times," Farley admitted. His arm tightened about Lorna.

"I'll be good," she promised. "I won't mention Judy any more."

However, later, when Greg asked her to dance, he brought the subject up again. Figuring this was as good a time as any, she asked his opinion on the idea of Judy being in the play.

"It's certainly worth trying," he agreed, smiling down at her. "Imagine you standing up to Judy's father! That took spunk." He grinned. "You're a pretty spunky little thing anyway. You almost let Marianne have it at the table."

"Was it that obvious?" She sighed. "No wonder Farley gets annoyed with me."

"You're good for him," Greg told her.

She felt her face grow warm and changed the subject. "Judy wants to be a nurse's aid. I wonder about eventually enrolling her in the practical nurses' training course at the Vocational School."

"If she's interested, it might be the best thing for her. We can follow the idea up, when she seems ready for it."

When the tempo of the music increased, she followed him into the faster step. Greg was a smooth and graceful dancer. By the time they returned to the table, Nola was preparing to leave. Marianne was protesting, "It's Friday night, what's the hurry?"

"I've got a family of six children to check on early in the morning," Nola explained, smiling.

"I've got to report in early too," Peter told them.

"Why don't we stay awhile?" Farley suggested.

Lorna shook her head. "I really think we should go. I've got to see—" Judy's name almost slipped out. "I've got to work tomorrow."

"And I suppose you do too?" Marianne asked Greg. "I guess everyone here works but little old me."

Lorna could not talk much with Farley on the way home because Nola and Peter were along. She had tried to be particularly pleasant to Marianne at parting; she hoped he had noticed it. She really should try to be nicer to his friends. It *was* boring, she supposed, for them to hear her talk about her work; but she was sometimes bored with his friends too. The thought struck her that his friends would be her friends when they were married. She sighed. But there were people like Greg and Mary Renlo . . . At least they weren't all like Marianne and Milli.

Chapter Eight

Lorna had asked Mrs. Hart to call a meeting of the Residence girls who were to take part in the play, and to bring Judy along. The meeting was to begin at six-thirty this evening, and it was almost four now. Lorna frowned at the script in front of her . . . would Judy accept the role that required her to play the piano during the performance?

For the past two weeks, since Mr. Stillman had permitted his daughter to remain at the Y all the time, Judy had shown some improvement, but progress was slower than Lorna and the Housemother had hoped for.

The flash of Lorna's diamond ring in the late afternoon sunshine reminded her that she had not spent as much extra time with the girl as she would have liked. It was not just the heavy workload that November had brought . . . there had been many social engagements that Farley insisted they keep. Dinners, the theater, dancing, and Mary Renlo's lovely party, which had been the nicest of all.

It was not that Lorna had neglected her work; but she had twinges of guilt because she could not attend many of the Y functions that she had organized. The group she felt badly about was the Golden Age Club for she seldom had time to attend their meetings. As Farley said, she could hardly be expected to work all the time. Why couldn't he be more understanding about her job? The other evening, for instance, the president of the Golden Age Club had personally asked her to attend their holiday dance. Noticing her engagement ring, he added, "Perhaps your young man would also like to come." When Lorna told Farley about the invitation, he had stared at her blankly.

"Oh come now, sugar. You're not really serious, are you?"

"I most certainly am. If you could see those sweet people, especially the ones over seventy. They're as lively as spring colts!"

"I'll bet," he replied unenthusiastically. "What would I do—pass cookies while you pour the tea? Or maybe you expect me to waltz with grandmother while you do a mazurka with grandpop?"

"Perhaps," she said, on the defensive now. "It would give them a wonderful lift and, who knows, you might even enjoy it. The dance is December 28. Save that night, will you, Farley?"

"I'll try to, sugar, but that's a long time from now."

She knew then that he did not plan to attend. In a way she couldn't blame him; it was so different from anything he had ever been asked to do. But he could be so charming, and, she had to admit, she would be proud to show him off.

The telephone on her desk rang. Sarah Snowden, the social worker from the Community House, was on the line. She was one of Lorna's favorites, a quiet, slender woman with graying brown hair and a fine understanding of people.

"I wonder if you have a room at the Y for one of the girls from our district? Her name is Lily Ricardo, and she has been living with her married sister. Last night there was an argument and the sister's husband told her to get out and stay out. She has no parents, no place to go."

"What caused the argument, Sarah?"

"I haven't had time to investigate the matter thoroughly, but I did call the sister. Naturally I couldn't learn much from her; she's torn between loyalty to Lily and to her husband."

"I think we can find space, but I'll check with Mrs. Hart. However, I'd like to know more about the situation, especially if she has to share a room with another girl."

"Lily has never been in trouble, if that's what you mean; and she has a job in a five-and-ten."

"Why don't you send her over and let me talk with her, Sarah?"

"Fine, I'll do that. I certainly hope you can help her, Lorna," Sarah said earnestly. "She can't afford an apartment, and with the holiday season coming up, it would be sad for her to be alone."

Half an hour later Lily appeared. She was a small girl with an abundance of black hair; in her sweater and skirt she looked about fifteen years old.

"Miss Snowden tells me you would like to live here, Lily?"

"Oh very much!"

"She also tells me you are employed. You've finished school then?" Lorna smiled to put the girl at her ease. She seemed very nervous.

"I didn't finish school. I wanted to, but . . . well, I didn't have clothes like the other girls, and it's hard being different—"

"Different?"

"I mean living different. You see, my brother-in-law came from the old country. He brought my sister over here when they got married. My sister is thirteen years older than me."

Lorna could understand that this age difference might be a problem, for her brother Nels was fifteen years older than she was, and a few years ago she had not understood him at all. "My sister and brother still live like in the old country," Lily continued, "but I don't want to live like that—I want to live American!" In her rebellion, Lily appeared older. "My brother-in-law and I, we fight all the time."

"He has given you a good home, hasn't he?" Lorna tried to keep her tone light and pleasant.

"He doesn't like me, though. He won't let me have any friends in the house. He won't let me do anything. That's why I went to work at the dime store, to get money to move out." An angry flush deepened her olive skin. "But he threw me out before I could save enough."

"Would you care to tell me why he threw you out, Lily?"

"Because a few friends came over while they were out and left me with the kids. It's the only time I can have anyone in."

"Girl friends?" Lorna asked casually.

"Just girls from the neighborhood." Lily's small shoulders twitched resentfully. "It's like I told you, he don't believe I should have any friends." Suddenly her resentment disappeared, and she put her hands on the desk, palms up. "If you don't let me come here, I'll have to ask him to take me back. Oh Miss Evans, you don't know how mean my brother-in-law is to me!" With a quick change of mood she exclaimed, "I won't go back, I'll get a room, on lower Broadway if I have to. I know where I can get one cheap."

It was an idle threat, Lorna felt sure. What could this child know of lower Broadway? But she undoubtedly would rather find a cheap room somewhere than go back home. "If you stay here, Lily, you must obey the rules."

"Oh yes, I know that."

Finally Lorna decided to take the girl to see Mrs. Hart and

let her fill out a Residence application form. Presently the Housemother came into Lorna's office. "Did you want Lily assigned to a permanent room?"

"Can you manage one?"

"I haven't a single room. I'll have to put her in with one of the other girls." She hesitated. "We don't know much about her. Usually we wait for references . . ."

"There isn't time for that now." Lorna told her about Sarah Snowden's call, and related Lily's version of the situation.

"Something about the story doesn't ring quite true," Mrs. Hart remarked thoughtfully. "I feel that we should know more about Lily, especially before putting her in with someone . . ." This wasn't like Mrs. Hart; she usually welcomed the girls with open arms. Surely she could see that Lily was in need of shelter.

"Sarah Snowden says she's never been in trouble," Lorna assured the Housemother.

"Nevertheless, she seems terribly nervous. Don't you think we should hear the brother-in-law's side of the story?"

"You're probably right, Mrs. Hart." Lorna was disturbed to find the woman so insistent. Why wouldn't the girl be nervous after being thrown out of the only home she ever had? "But there's no time to do any checking now. We can look into the matter next week. Meanwhile, Lily will have a place to stay, at least temporarily."

"Well, on that basis, I think it will be all right. I can put her in with Jennifer Lawrence, who is about the same age."

"Fine. Jennifer's a quiet girl and she'll probably be a good influence, if Lily stays on."

Sitting alone in her office, Lorna wondered if she had done the right thing. Although the Housemother was not a trained worker, her instinct about these things was usually reliable. In any case, nothing serious could happen in a few days, and Lily's story could be checked later. Actually, there seemed little reason to worry; Miss Snowden had not indicated any doubts and Lily *was* appealing . . .

That evening when Lorna arrived at the meeting of the play cast, Lenore Coleman, Sally Williams and Betty Morton—the girls who had been so concerned about Judy the evening she had hidden herself in the bathroom—were already there. Lorna was glad for a chance to talk with them before Judy came. "Do you remember," she asked, "that you told me you would like to help Judy?"

"We meant it, too," Sally said. "She's doing better though; the other day she showed me a dress she made. I wish I could sew like that!"

"Why don't you ask her to teach you?" Mrs. Hart suggested, entering the room at that moment.

"I'd love to have her teach me too," Betty piped up. "But usually when I try to talk to her, she clams up."

"I'm sure she'd help you," Mrs. Hart said. "It would be the best thing for her if she would."

"Judy wants to take up nursing," Lorna explained, "but before she can go to school, she must overcome her shyness. I believe that if we could convince her to accept a part in the play, it would be a real beginning." The girls looked at her in surprise, so she added, "One can forget oneself when acting out a role."

"I bet we couldn't get Judy to say a word for love or money!" Sally announced.

Lorna turned the pages of the script slowly. "I thought she might take the part of the pianist. She would have nothing to say, and she plays beautifully."

"She certainly does," Lenore agreed. "I heard her playing

in the lounge the other night when she thought no one was around."

"Do you think she will do it, Mrs. Hart?" Betty asked.

"Why don't I go and ask her?" Mrs. Hart got up, smiling. At the door she held up her hand, the first two fingers crossed, and the three girls crossed theirs too.

A few minutes later the Housemother returned with Judy in tow. She was wearing the new dress she had made and her shining hair was brushed back from her face and curled softly at the nape of her neck. Lorna greeted her warmly and received a shy smile in return. She moved over on the couch and Judy quietly sat down beside her. The rest of the cast arrived and the discussion began.

"One of our problems," Mrs. Hart said, "is that we need someone to play the piano. Lenore is taking the part of the office girl, and she's the only one who knows how to play." Bless her, Lorna thought, she was making it all sound so natural.

Lenore looked up innocently. "Judy can play the piano. I heard her the other night."

Judy shrank back against the couch. "I've never been in a play," she whispered, her eyes growing wider with alarm.

"It's easy." Sally put a handkerchief on her head, turned up her white collar. "I'm the maid; this is my cap. You see, it's like being someone else, a masquerade." She walked around the room, holding an imaginary tray. "Champagne, Madame?" she chirped as she bobbed her head at each girl. Everyone burst into laughter, and even Judy smiled faintly at Sally's antics.

"Remember when you went trick-or-treating?" Betty offered. "You weren't afraid. You were that witch or ghost or whatever costume you had on."

"I never went trick-or-treating," Judy said in a small voice.

"Never?" Sally was incredulous.

"Lots of kids don't," Lenore put in quietly. Lorna had not been aware of how sensitive the girl was; but then, she did not see much of the girls except during group activities or when they came to her with problems.

"All you'd have to do is to play the piano," Mrs. Hart explained. "You'd just come out and sit down at the piano as if you were all alone in the room."

Judy looked appealingly at Lorna. "If you think I should . . . I'll try."

"Wonderful!" Mrs. Hart got up. "Would you like to help me cut the cake while the other parts are being assigned?"

Judy got up. Without looking to right or left, she went to the kitchen. But when she returned with the cake, Lorna noticed that she appeared more relaxed and happy.

The first rehearsal was set for December 2, giving the girls time to learn their parts. When there was not a crumb of cake or a drop of coffee left, the group broke up, declaring that it had been a most successful meeting.

Several days later Mrs. Hart came into Lorna's office, her serene face uncharacteristically worried. "I'd like to talk with you about Grace Walker, the colored girl who moved into the Residence two weeks ago. The girls aren't accepting her, and we can't understand it. We have had colored girls before and they've always fitted in well. Remember Marcia Beaman who left in August? She was one of the most popular girls we've ever had."

"We have another colored girl in the Residence now, haven't we?" Lorna asked.

The Housemother nodded. "Mabel Parsons."

"I've met her at several of the social functions at the

Residence, and as far as I could see, she was well liked by the girls."

"Oh yes, she is. In fact, I think that may be part of the trouble: Mabel has made no effort to make friends with Grace, and this may explain the others' indifference to the new girl. If Mabel ignores her, perhaps they think something's wrong with Grace. The fact is that she's a very nice girl and is having a rather hard time of it right now. Being new in the city, she has no other friends and doesn't want to force herself on anyone here."

"It must be rough on her," Lorna agreed. "But I'm sure that there is something we can do to help. First of all, I think I should have a talk with Mabel."

Mrs. Hart smiled in relief. "I was hoping you'd say that. It's certainly the most direct approach. Mabel is in her room now, if you have some free time."

Lorna got up at once. "There's nothing pressing at the moment—I'll just tell Bea where I'm going."

As they headed toward the Residence section Mrs. Hart asked, "Have you done any further checking on Lily Ricardo?"

There was a moment's awkward silence as Lorna searched for an answer. "Well, no," she began, feeling somewhat remiss. "I've been so rushed this past week, I just haven't gotten around to it. Has anything happened?"

"Oh no, it's not that," Mrs. Hart replied. "She and Jennifer seem to be getting along fine. But I still can't help feeling worried. Jennifer has been such a quiet girl who never seemed to want to go out much. In the short time that Lily has been here, she has somehow managed to get Jennifer to go out almost every evening."

"Where do they go?"

"Apparently just downtown to window-shop, have a hamburger somewhere or go to a movie . . ."

"Well, there's no harm in that, Mrs. Hart. I suspect that Jennifer is a very shy girl and just needed someone to befriend her. Lily's such a lively type, no one could sit and mope when she's around."

Although the Housemother made no further comment, it was obvious that she still felt an investigation was necessary.

"I'll call Lily's sister this afternoon and arrange to see her as soon as possible," Lorna promised as she turned down the corridor that led to Mabel Parsons' room.

"Are you busy, or may I come in for a moment?" she asked when Mabel answered the knock at her door. "Oh, how charming this is!" she exclaimed as she stepped inside. "I haven't seen your room before, Mabel—these personal touches give it such a warmth." She paused to admire a large still-life painting, then walked over to the window. "I love this inside window-box arrangement of plants . . . was this your idea or did you see it in a magazine?"

"Both, actually. I had to do a little improvising, but I guess it turned out pretty well. Won't you sit down, Miss Evans?"

Lorna chose the straight-back chair next to the small desk-table and waited for Mabel to seat herself, noting how attractive she was, with expressive brown eyes and a low, well-modulated voice.

"You're a trained nurse, aren't you, Mabel?"

"Yes, at the Tacoma General Hospital."

"I understand that you're very happy in your work," Lorna said.

Mabel nodded. "Very. It was something I always wanted to do."

"I know how you feel—I wanted to do social work. In a way, the two professions are alike, don't you agree?"

"I suppose they are." Mabel regarded Lorna thoughtfully.

"I was wondering if you've met one of our new girls yet, Grace Walker?" Lorna asked, leading into the subject casually.

"Yes, several times. Why do you ask, Miss Evans?"

"Mrs. Hart mentioned that she hasn't made any friends here. It occurs to me that it must be very lonely for her."

"Most girls probably are lonely when they first arrive," Mabel said quietly, but there was a noticeable change in her manner. "It takes time, you know."

"I haven't overlooked that fact, but it also takes something more than *time*: it takes *people* and the small effort required to make somone feel accepted, at home . . ." Lorna's voice trailed off as Mabel stood up and walked across the room. She stared out the window a few moments, then turned around abruptly.

"Just what are you trying to say, Miss Evans?"

Lorna looked directly at her. "It's part of my job to see that the girls are happy here, Mabel, and frankly I was hoping that you might be able to tell me why Grace hasn't made friends with anyone."

"How should I know? Her room is at the other end of the building and I see very little of her."

"Nevertheless, you've been here some time and—"

"And we're of the same race, is that it?" Mabel broke in, her tone icy.

"That's partly it," Lorna replied honestly, but she was distressed at the way the conversation was going. "It certainly is one reason why you might be willing to help her."

"Just because we are both colored doesn't mean that we have to be buddy-buddy. The girl's face looked strained and she was on the defensive now. "I don't have to associate with everyone of my race any more than you have to in yours. Grace and I have very little in common—our interests, our backgrounds, are not the same."

"That may very well be the case, but I wonder if that's the real reason, Mabel. After all, that girl is new, she's lonely, she doesn't want to push her way into the group. Would you feel the same way toward her if she weren't colored?" Studying Mabel's face, Lorna knew that she had touched upon the truth.

"No, I suppose I wouldn't. But look, Miss Evans, I've been here for almost a year now and I've worked hard to make friends. I'm accepted now . . . but if I suddenly began to associate with Grace, everyone would say, 'They're alike, they have each other.' More and more they'd leave us alone, and both Grace and I would wind up being excluded. Oh, it wouldn't be intentional, mind you—but the effect is the same, isn't it?" She turned back to the window as her voice broke. "No thanks, Miss Evans. Let her make her own friends, the way I did."

It was the first time that Lorna had ever considered this aspect of the situation, and she did not know how to reply. Perhaps Mabel's fears were justified. On the other hand, the girl could not go through life ignoring people of her own race because she was afraid to lose the friends she had made in another.

"I'm sorry, Mabel; I know that this conversation is painful to you, but I hope you realize that it is for me too," Lorna began gently. "There are undoubtedly many things I cannot fully appreciate or understand about this problem, and very likely there are aspects that you cannot see. For instance, perhaps you are not giving yourself and your friends at the Y enough credit. If the liking is genuine on both sides, why should your kindness to Grace affect it? After all, I'm not suggesting that you and she become inseparable; I'm merely asking you not to ignore her completely so that the other girls won't think there's something wrong with her and pay no attention to her. Is that an unreasonable request?"

"Perhaps not, but I still feel she should find her own way to fit in," Mabel replied shortly.

Lorna looked down at her hands. "No one finds her way completely on her own—somebody has to give a little on the other side. What about your own case—didn't Marcia Beaman invite you to join the choral group shortly after you arrived?" Lorna saw that this point hit home.

Mabel sank down on the edge of the bed. "You win, Miss Evans. I guess I'd forgotten about that. Grace may think that the girls here are prejudiced, but it looks as if I'm the one who is—the only one . . ."

"Well, at times none of us sees things too clearly.

"It's hard to be sure about prejudice though. I mean one is always on guard against slights—which may only be imagined—if there is a difference of color." Mabel seemed a bit more relaxed now.

"It's not only a question of color, Mabel. A tall girl blames her height if she goes to a party and only one person asks her for a dance. If a fat girl isn't popular she blames it on her weight. Actually, those may not be the reasons at all—or she hasn't learned to cope with those problems, minimize them, and develop her other assets." Lorna could not help wondering if she sounded like some Voice of Experience, and she wondered what Farley would think if he could hear her now.

"I guess I'm still on the defensive more than I care to admit," Mabel said with a rueful smile. "The other day I was in a restaurant downtown and I waited a half-hour without anyone coming to take my order. I was convinced that it was because I was colored, and I got up and left. Just as I got to the door, some white people behind me were complaining that the service was so slow they couldn't wait any longer. I felt a little foolish, but it is so easy to blame such things on the color of one's skin . . ."

Lorna was quiet for a moment, thinking. "It's curious how we sometimes lean over in the opposite direction. A couple of summers ago I was at a camp which had brought a music director, a Negro college student, from the East. One of the counselors went so far out of his way to be a jolly good fellow and prove his friendliness that he embarrassed the director and everyone else in camp. It got so the poor guy couldn't even go to his room to read quietly instead of taking a five-mile hike up a mountainside, lest he offend the counselor!"

Mabel could not help laughing at the story. "You've really been very kind to me, Miss Evans," she said as Lorna stood up to leave. "It's all too easy to have these misunderstandings, which grow worse and worse unless they can be talked out frankly—the way we did just now."

"I'm very glad I came," Lorna replied. "I'm sure we can all find a way to help one another, if each is willing to give a little bit more."

She did not press Mabel further about helping Grace Walker. It was best to give her time to think about the situation, and let her make the next move if and when she reached a decision. Lorna was certain that Mabel would decide in favor of the new girl.

That night after a movie she told Farley about the episode. "The trouble was," she explained, "I wasn't thinking of it from the viewpoint of the individuals concerned, I was thinking of it from the viewpoint of race, and that was wrong, Farley."

"Everyone is a member of a race, sugar."

"Yes, but first they are individuals, and it is as such that we must view them."

"Why trouble your pretty head about it?" He slipped his arm around her. "This race problem has been with us for generations."

"But it must be settled. Surely it's time we gave it serious consideration."

"So a couple of girls at the Y aren't friendly with each other! Why get all upset? People all over the world are having their little spats—"

"People all over the world are having their big spats too, and big spats lead to war. What kind of prestige does it give us in the world if we can't treat our own people as first-class citizens, if we can't give a little thought to their problems?"

"Honey"—he leaned over and kissed her lightly on the temple—"smarter heads than ours are pondering this problem. I don't think we can settle it tonight, and furthermore I don't think we should try. Look at that moon!" His arm would have pulled her close, but she drew back.

"I'm really serious about this, Farley. Problems between races will be solved not by great minds, but by people like you and me, in whatever small ways we can find to lessen the gap between ourselves and people of other races."

"It isn't such a big problem . . ."

"How can you say that? How would you like someone to tell you where you could walk and eat, what college you could attend, and draw a line as to the station you could aspire to in life?"

"Look, Lorna, if you're going to spend our last five minutes tonight lecturing me on racial equality, I'd just as soon walk you right up to that door."

"That's okay with me!" She opened the door on her own side of the car and jumped out. She had gone only a few steps when he caught up with her. "And it isn't just a matter of a couple of girls at the Y.W.C.A. either!" she flared at him.

"All right, sugar, let's drop it then." But she would not let him kiss her goodnight.

"Please don't, Farley, not tonight. I've got lots of things on my mind and you're no help."

She left him standing there in the lobby, looking after her. The apartment was lonely, quiet and she tiptoed over to close the bedroom door so she would not disturb Nola, who was sound asleep. These differences with Farley would have to be settled before they were married—it would be too late afterward. The thought kept crowding itself into her mind that perhaps they could not be settled . . . How could she be sure?

Suddenly she had an overwhelming desire to talk to her parents. Surely they could comfort her, reassure her. She made up her mind and scribbled a note to them, saying she would be down to visit them at Thanksgiving. Farley had been coaxing her to stay in Tacoma and attend all the parties that their friends were planning. Until now she had been undecided about going away for the long week-end, but tonight her mind was made up. Lest she be tempted to change it, she put on her coat again, ran downstairs and slipped the letter into the corner postbox.

Chapter Nine

"I still don't see why you have to go to your brother's for this holiday," Farley grumbled as he drove Lorna to the airport. "Why didn't you tell your family you'd see them at Christmastime?"

"We've been all through that," she replied wearily. "I *want* to see them now; there are lots of things to talk over with them before we can settle our own plans. You keep asking me to set a date for the wedding—well, when I get back we'll decide."

Farley said in that case the trip was worth it, and let the subject drop. "Have fun," he told her as he kissed her goodby before she boarded the jet.

In two hours she was being welcomed by her mother, father and an assortment of nieces and nephews. Nels picked up her suitcase and started for the car, and the rest of them followed, with everybody talking at once.

The three-day holiday passed all too quickly and Lorna enjoyed every minute of it. She found her mother happy in her new surroundings, helping with the children, baking, sewing, and keeping busy as usual. Her father, however, did not have much to occupy him, and he was growing restless.

His one pleasure was Nels' small garden, in which he puttered around every day.

Naturally, the first thing everybody wanted to hear about was Lorna's engagement and her young man.

"That's quite a diamond," her brother said in surprise. "He must have quite a lot of money to buy that for you."

"Do you have any pictures of him?" Betty, his wife, wanted to know. As she inspected the snapshots Lorna handed her, she whistled. "He's handsome, isn't he? How did you meet him?"

"What does this young fellow do?" her father asked, which was the sort of question Lorna expected of him.

"I'm sure he must be a very fine young man if our Lorna has fallen in love with him," her mother announced quietly. "I was wondering if you two have discussed the possibility of your continuing to work—I mean on the same basis. He probably wouldn't want you to have a job, but you could do volunteer work."

"Oh, I don't intend to stop, Mother—I couldn't give up social work," Lorna declared firmly.

Nels stopped puffing on his pipe long enough to say, "I don't see why not."

Before Lorna could reply, Betty added, "Marriage is a full-time job, as you'll soon find out." Her happy face was proof that she had no objections to it either.

It was not until Sunday morning that Lorna had the opportunity to discuss the situation privately with her mother. Mrs. Evans came directly to the point.

"Why do you want to wait almost a year before getting married, dear? And why all this insistence upon continuing to have a full-time job afterward?"

"There are lots of reasons, Mother. For one thing, I love

my work. But I also want to return the money you spent on my education."

"That's very sweet of you, Lorna, and I'm not denying that we could use it. But your father and I don't want that to interfere with your happiness. We can manage, you know. Nels wants us to move down here and he can help us out a little."

"Well, maybe you should live here—the warmer climate is better for both of you. But in any case, I *want* to pay you back. Farley has offered to give me the money after we're married, but I can't let him do it. That's my responsibility. You think I'm right, don't you? You agree with me?" Lorna asked anxiously.

Her mother did not answer immediately as she searched her daughter's face. "I'm not sure that I do, dear," she finally said. "If we sell our house in Seattle, it will relieve our financial worries temporarily and your father is sure that he can get some kind of part-time job here to add to his small pension. We certainly appreciate your desire to help, Lorna, but we don't want to stand in your way." She hesitated before continuing. "Are you sure that you are not using this as an excuse?"

Lorna looked unhappily at her mother. "I—I'm not sure," she whispered. "I've asked myself that question over and over. Farley and I are so different . . . we see so many things differently . . . Did you and Dad have this problem?" She was very close to tears now.

"All married couples have to make adjustments, dear, because no two people see eye to eye on everything. Fortunately, your father and I were able to work things out without too much difficulty, and our backgrounds were similar. You can't expect Farley to understand how you feel about working and helping those who are in trouble; he's never had to worry about money, meeting bills, paying debts . . ." Mrs. Evans took her daughter's hand, not knowing how to comfort her. "I cannot tell you whether you are right for each other. I can only tell you that if you love one another, you can solve your differences in time. But you must be sure, in your own heart, that you love and want to marry him."

Just then Nels walked into the room. "Time for lunch, you two," he announced. "You can continue your little chat later."

But there was no chance to talk to her mother again, and Lorna got on the plane that evening with her doubts still unresolved. She was glad that she had come, but parting from her family was very painful. Even Farley's obvious delight at seeing her when she walked through the gates at the Tacoma airport did not dispel the sadness she felt.

"I missed you, sugar," he told her as he started the car. "I won't let you go away without me again. How were your folks?"

Lorna knew he had been disappointed that she had not asked him to join her family for Thanksgiving, but she had not wanted him to meet them just yet. Had she been afraid that he would be critical of their modest way of life? she asked herself.

"Everyone's fine," she replied. "Of course it was pretty hectic, with four young children in the house, but it was good to see Mom and Dad again."

He reached over and squeezed her hand. "Now that you've seen your folks, we can settle the question. When's the big day going to be, sugar?"

"Oh Farley, I'm so tired, it's been quite a busy week end for me," she fenced. "Let's talk about it after I've had some rest, okay?"

"I've made a reservation at the Cliff House for dinner tomorrow night. All that candlelight and sweet music will put you in the mood, sugar. Not even Lorna Evans can resist that romantic atmosphere!"

He held her close before letting her get out of the car in front of her apartment house. "Until tomorrow," he murmured, pressing his lips to hers.

Monday was a difficult day at work for Lorna. There was a stack of correspondence on her desk, waiting to be answered, and phone calls kept interrupting her as she tried to concentrate on the letters she was writing.

Promptly at five o'clock she cleared her desk and left the office, anxious to get home and relax for an hour before getting ready for her date. "I don't know why I should be so nervous," she told herself, but she could not get rid of the uneasiness that overwhelmed her.

Farley was charming and attentive all during dinner, making no mention of the subject she was dreading to discuss. But as they lingered over coffee, he brought it up.

"Okay, sugar. I told Mother and Dad we'd drop in after we leave here and give them the word. I'll bet there's champagne on ice right now, just waiting to be opened as soon as we announce the date."

Lorna took a deep breath. "We can't be married for at least a year, Farley, so you really shouldn't have said anything to your family."

"A year? What in heaven do we have to wait that long for?"

"I've told you, I have to pay back the money I owe my parents. Oh, I knew you said you'd take care of it, but I can't let you."

"Now look, Lorna, that's ridiculous. You'll be my wife. What's wrong with my paying them?"

"Nothing *wrong*—it's just that I can't accept your offer."

"You mean you *won't*. I don't understand your attitude, sugar. Do you want to marry me or not?"

"Of course . . . but the point is, you don't understand me, how I feel about the money, about my work—"

"Okay, okay," he interrupted her impatiently. "If you want to work after we're married, I won't stop you. I'm not going to let a little thing like that keep—"

It was Lorna's turn to interrupt him. "Little thing, you call it! It just happens to be the most important thing in my life!"

"So it seems." Farley's voice was edged with impatience. "It's all you ever talk about."

"You don't have to listen," she told him angrily. "I've spent six years training for this work and I'm not going to give it up after a few short months. I want to help people and be of some use in this world."

"That's a lot of idealism!" he snapped. "We'd better get this straight once and for all: I don't want my wife meddling around in other people's lives. After we're married you will have everything you could possibly want. You can help your folks out any way you want to. After a while we'll have kids—you said you wanted a family—and you'll have other interests to make you forget all this Pollyanna stuff."

Lorna stared at him. "Is that what you think of my work—meddling, Pollyanna stuff? Would you prefer that I amuse myself by giving little bridge luncheons in the afternoon and getting all dressed up in Paris creations to attend a constant round of parties in the evening? Well, that's not what I want out of life!"

As they sat in angry silence, avoiding each other's eyes, a rustle of silk and a bubbling voice suddenly caught their attention. Lorna looked up to see Milli Mercer and Jerry Lester standing by their table.

"Well look who's here! The lovebirds enjoying a little *tête-à-tête!*" Milli warbled.

"Oh hi, Milli. We've just finished dinner and we're leaving; otherwise I'd ask you to join us," Farley said with a forced smile.

"That's all right, sweetie. We're joining some friends over there—" Milli waved her hand vaguely—"but I just wanted to say hello and tell you I expect an invitation to your wedding. It will be the biggest social event of the spring."

Lorna did not even try to be cordial. "And who told you it was going to be this spring?"

"Farley, of course, darling. Although why you're waiting *that* long is beyond me. You're taking a big chance, letting such an eligible bachelor run around loose!"

"You're overrating me, Milli," Farley said, not giving Lorna a chance to make any reply. "But don't worry about an invitation—you'll get one."

"I hope so . . . I wouldn't want to miss kissing the bridegroom—or is it the bride? Oh, well, it doesn't matter. Come along, Jerry, our friends are waiting. Nice to see you two." Milli floated off, with Jerry in her wake.

As soon as they were out of earshot Lorna looked across the table. "Why have you been telling everybody that the wedding is set for the spring? Couldn't you at least have waited until we talked it over?"

Farley's face had a determined expression. "Listen, Lorna, those were my friends and they've all been asking. I feel like a fool telling them I don't know. Just what did you expect me to say?"

"I wouldn't have cared what you told them, if only you hadn't made it so definite."

The waiter approached, and Farley signaled for the check. "We can continue our discussion in the car. This is really not the place to talk anyway."

Lorna waited until they were on their way back to town before she spoke again. "Why is it that we always seem to get into arguments about my job? I don't want it to be a problem, but I can no longer pretend to myself that it isn't."

"I guess it's just that I love you, sugar, and I hate to see you get so involved in all those miserable cases, which you take so seriously. We're young and we should be thinking about all the fun we can have together. I was going to tell you earlier that I've decided to take some time off from the shop so we can go to Europe for our honeymoon." He gave her a quick smile. "When we get back there'll be lots for you to do: buy furniture, decorate our home, plan parties and dinners for our friends to celebrate our homecoming. And of course I have a position to maintain in the community—business obligations to meet as well as social ones. Between all those things and whatever charity work you want to do, you won't have much time on your hands, sugar."

Lorna made no response, and Farley kept glancing at her worriedly. "Haven't you anything to say?" he finally asked.

"There's nothing to say, I'm afraid. You have it all figured out—except for one thing: I wouldn't be happy leading the life you've planned for yourself."

"And I suppose you think you'd be happy looking after a bunch of tramps and mixed-up delinquents!" Farley's hand gripped the wheel tightly as he rasped out the words.

"Call them anything you want—it doesn't change the fact that they need help and I intend to give it, if I can. If you can't accept the way I am, I'm afraid there's no hope for us," Lorna answered wearily, but she knew that she meant every word she said.

"Come on, sugar, let's not make a mountain out of a mole-hill." They had reached the city and Farley stopped for a red light. "Let's go and spend an hour or so with my folks. They want very much to see you again; besides, we need a chance to relax and cool off."

"Thank you, Farley, but I'd prefer to go straight home. You don't seem to realize that there is a mountain between us—a high one—and it will always be there. I think I've always known it, but I didn't want to admit it. There's no point in going on with this."

"You don't know what you're saying, Lorna." Farley sounded alarmed. "You love me, you've told me so. And I love you. Surely that means something to you."

"Perhaps what we feel isn't enough," she replied, and tears began to choke her voice. "Love is respecting each other's beliefs, sharing dreams, building something more than castles in the air. We don't have that . . ."

As the car pulled up at the curb by her apartment, she turned to him. "I can't marry you, Farley."

"Don't talk like that, Lorna; I won't let you go." He tried to put his arms around her but she pulled back.

"No, Farley. Here's your ring . . . it's best that we end it now. I could never make you happy—not really." Tears streamed down her face as she took off the ring. When he refused to take it, she put it on the seat beside him.

"Good-by . . . ," she whispered, opening the door. "Please don't come in with me."

"Lorna, don't go——" His voice broke, but she would not look back.

"Lorna . . ."

Blindly she ran into the lobby and up the stairs, trying to shut out his voice calling her name. She refused to answer the buzzer, which rang insistently several times. When it stopped, she flung her coat off and threw herself on her bed, weeping bitterly.

Sobs were still racking her body half an hour later when the shrill sound of the telephone shattered the dark silence of the living room. Lorna burrowed her head in the pillow, praying for the phone to stop before she weakened and answered it. There was a brief pause, then it began to ring again, and this time it kept on and on until she thought she could stand it no longer. Finally she raised herself on the bed and was about to go out and pick up the receiver, because she so desperately wanted to hear Farley's voice telling her that he loved her, needed her . . . But the ringing stopped. The phone did not ring again and Lorna lay awake in the dark, saying to herself, "It's over, over, over . . ."

Lorna never knew how she got through the rest of that week. During the day it was not so bad, for her counseling schedule was so full that she had little time to dwell on her own problems. In addition, the various club and class activities had reached their peak, and for each group there were plans to consider, decisions to make, final arrangements to be settled. In a way, she was grateful for the distraction her job provided, and she plunged into the work with furious energy.

But the evenings were quite a different matter. The long, lonely hours of each night dragged by, with nothing to do but sit and think. A hundred times she asked herself if she had done the right thing; a hundred times the answer came back: there could be no other way. Why, then, did she ache so? She missed Farley terribly, yet each time he called she refused to see him. It would do no good, she told him.

She had not given Nola any details about the breakup of her engagement, and the other girl was too discreet to ask questions. Her sympathy was evident, but she did not try to force it on Lorna.

"Want to go to the movies with me tonight?" she asked as they were fixing dinner on Wednesday.

"I'd rather not, if you don't mind," Lorna replied. "But thanks for asking."

"I understand, pet. I won't be out late; I have some letters to write when I get back. By the way, I left a new magazine on the coffee table. It's full of suggestions for Christmas gifts. Perhaps we can look at it together, if you're starting your list early. Personally, I'm fresh out of ideas."

"Every year I promise myself I'll do my shopping early, but I always end up in a last-minute rush." Lorna suddenly dreaded the thought of the holiday season, with no Farley to brighten it . . . But she mustn't think about that. "I think maybe I'll read awhile and go to bed early. I'm bushed."

Realizing that Lorna preferred to be left alone, Nola did not press the matter further.

The next afternoon Lorna was sitting in her office, making out a case report, when the phone rang. Her heart leaped as she answered it. Could it be Farley . . . ?

"Miss Evans? Greg Taylor calling. How are you?"

"Oh hello! I'm quite well, thank you. It's been some time since we spoke." It was surprisingly pleasant to hear his voice.

"I know; I was just thinking the same thing, so I thought I'd call and see how Judy Stillman is coming along. Is she going to appear in that play, or did she drop out?"

"She's been attending all the rehearsals, so we have our fingers crossed that she won't back out at the last minute. Until this week she was doing fine, but now she's beginning to show signs of weakening. It would be a real setback if she refused to go on, after all this."

"I wouldn't worry too much about that, if I were you. By the way, what night is the play? I'd like to see it."

"It's next Friday, and if you're serious about coming, I'll send you two tickets."

"I seldom say things I don't mean, Lorna; and I'll only need one ticket. You'll be there, of course?"

"Naturally; I wouldn't miss it for anything."

"Neither would I. See you then."

"Good-by, Greg." How different he was from Farley, who had told her he couldn't be bothered sitting through such an "amateur" performance. Amateur or not, it meant a great deal to the girls at the Y, but she could never have explained that to him.

Lorna looked down at the bare third finger of her left hand. Farley could never change, nor could she—that was what she had written in a letter to her parents.

The following Friday Lorna left work early to go home and change. Upon her return to the Y around seven, she was told that Mrs. Hart was anxious to see her.

"Thank heavens you're back!" the Housemother exclaimed as soon as she saw her. "Judy has locked herself in her room and won't come out."

"Oh no! I was praying that something like this wouldn't happen." Lorna tried to remain calm. "We must find a way to make her open the door . . . and I think I know how. Do you have a pair of scissors?"

Mrs. Hart gave her a puzzled look but went to her sewing box. "Here," she said, "but what on earth are you going to do?"

Before answering, Lorna pried open several inches of the side seam of her skirt. Then she took a deep breath. "Let's hope that this works! I'm going down to her room now."

There was no time to lose, for the cast was already assembling backstage to put on make-up and arrange last-minute details of their costumes.

"Judy," Lorna called, rapping firmly on the girl's door. "Judy, are you there? This is Miss Evans and I need your help." There was silence inside the room and Lorna knocked again. "My dress is ripped, Judy. Would you please sew it for me? I can't go into the auditorium like this." She listened carefully and heard a slight movement inside. Then the door slowly opened. Judy stood there, her face tear-stained.

"Come in, Miss Evans," she whispered. "What happened?"

"Oh, I don't know—I just discovered this big opening in the seam of this dress. Look!" Lorna held the skirt out to one side. "Isn't that awful?"

"It's not so bad," Judy said a little less timidly. "I can sew that up for you in a couple of minutes."

"Would you? I'd be terribly grateful." She sat down on the edge of the bed while Judy got a needle and thread. "I don't know what I would have done if you hadn't been here. And you do such beautiful work."

"Thank you," the girl said softly as she bent over her sewing. "This is a very pretty dress, Miss Evans. I saw one almost like it in *Charm* magazine. They have some nice styles and I've been thinking I'd like to send for a pattern and make one of them."

Lorna was surprised that Judy was taking such an interest in fashions and dressmaking—it was a good sign. But why was she so upset about tonight's performance? Lorna decided to ask no questions, but wait and see what developed. They chatted a few minutes while Judy finished resewing the seam.

Then Lorna stood up and walked over to the mirror to smooth down her skirt. "You did a wonderful job, Judy.

Thank you." She glanced at her watch. "Goodness, it's getting late; we'd better be joining the others backstage."

Without hesitation or protest, the girl picked up a sheet of music, her copy of the script, and followed Lorna.

"I forgot to tell you that the nurses'-aid training program at the Vocational School begins after Christmas and I think you may be able to join one of the classes."

"Really? Do you think I should, Miss Evans? Maybe I'm too slow . . . I bungle things . . ."

"You certainly didn't bungle this seam, and I've seen some other work you've done. I have absolutely no doubt that you'll make a fine nurse's aid, Judy. And remember, being fast is not as important as being thorough."

"I guess you're right, but I'm so afraid I'll be a—a flop." Judy's voice failed her.

"I don't think you have to be afraid of that. Mrs. Hart and Dr. Marlow don't think so either. And you trust us, don't you?"

"Yes . . ."

By that time they had reached the auditorium, where the Housemother was anxiously waiting for them.

As Lorna stopped to speak to her, she heard Judy gasp. "He's going to watch the play!"

Following the girl's gaze, she saw Mr. Stillman coming down the hall.

"Isn't that nice?" Mrs. Hart said casually. "Too bad the parents of some of the other girls couldn't see them; many live too far away. Judy, I think we need your help with a couple of the costumes. Want to come to the dressing room with me?"

Judy stood there, irresolute, until Lorna spoke up. "That's an excellent idea. Poor Sally Benson is having trouble with her dress, but I think you'll know what to do." She watched them head down the aisle, then turned to see where Mr. Stillman was going to sit. Why did he have to turn up tonight? She wondered. Judy might refuse to walk out on stage, knowing her father was in the audience. As she looked around the auditorium, which was filling up quickly, she caught sight of Greg Taylor and Reverend Marlow.

"Good evening, Miss Evans," the minister said as she approached. "How's our protégée doing?"

"I'm not sure—now."

"Is anything wrong?" Greg asked quickly.

Lorna sighed. "Judy just saw her father as she was going backstage. She was very upset and I don't know how she's going to react. We can hardly ask him to leave, but his presence here might ruin everything."

"Why don't you go and see how she is, meanwhile I'll have a word with Mr. Stillman," Greg suggested.

Reverend Marlow went with him and Lorna hurried down the aisle. A few minutes later, while she was talking to Judy in the wings, Greg appeared.

"Hi there, young lady, making your debut tonight?"

Judy nodded shyly.

"I just ran into your father out there." Greg spoke as if she had not known it. "He's very proud of you tonight, and told me that he has missed your playing."

"Really?" Judy's eyes widened in disbelief. "He never used to like to hear me."

"Well, he gave me a message for you—he said he'd like you to play his favorite song tonight."

Judy grew excited. "He said that? Where is he?" She walked over to the curtain and peeped out at the audience. "Oh! Oh dear! There are an *awful* lot of people out there . . . I don't think I can play for them . . . For anyone . . ."

"You don't want to disappoint all your friends, or your

father, or Dr. Marlow, do you?" Lorna asked gently. "They came especially to hear you."

"Did Dr. Marlow really come? He said he would but I was sure he'd be too busy. I'd hate to disappoint *him* . . ."

A buzzer sounded—it was five minutes till curtain time.

"We'll see you later, Judy," Greg said. "Remember, this is your big night!" He took Lorna's arm and led her firmly down the short flight of stairs to the auditorium. "There's no point in your staying there, you know. She must learn to do things on her own. What she needs is self-confidence—which she'll never get if she doesn't try her own wings. Why don't we find a couple of seats together and watch how it goes?"

"Do you think she'll go through with it?" Lorna whispered as they sat down. The house lights were beginning to dim.

"I hope so. It's hard to tell about these things, but we have to take a chance on it."

Judy was to make her appearance near the end of the first act, and as the time drew near, Lorna could hardly bear the suspense. Sensing her tension, Greg reached out and patted her arm reassuringly. Suddenly the stage was empty. The lights were low—the moment had come.

Like a frightened fawn, Judy made her entrance, pausing for one breathless instant before continuing on her way to the piano. Seating herself, she slowly raised her hands and began to play, softly at first then louder and louder until the music swelled, filled the auditorium with a great dramatic crescendo. For her, there was no audience, there was no stage —only she and the music existed.

As the last notes faded away, Judy sank back, head bowed, until the first burst of applause ended. When she stood up, the clapping began again and this time she acknowledged the ovation with a bow and a shy smile.

Greg and Lorna applauded happily. "You see, there was nothing to worry about after all," he whispered.

Both of them glanced around to note Mr. Stillman's reaction, and Lorna was surprised at the expression of gentleness that softened his features. Why, he doesn't look *at all* like a great big shaggy bear! she thought.

Twice more Judy came on, and though she still seemed nervous, she did not falter. And when the play was over, the girls from the Residence flocked around to congratulate her. At the edge of the circle stood Mr. Stillman. Reverend Marlow came toward him, shook his hand, and then called Judy's name. The girl looked up, saw the minister, and smiled. Then she looked at her father. The pride and happiness in his face was so evident that, with no hesitation, she went to him.

Considerably cheered by the successful outcome of the evening, Lorna invited Greg into the library for coffee.

"I feel that Judy is just about ready for school now, don't you?" Lorna asked him.

"I'm sure she is. You've done wonders with her."

"I can't take all the credit, Greg. Mrs. Hart has spent a great deal of time with her; her motherly nature has been an important factor in Judy's improvement. And you have been a big help to us too."

"You like your work very much, don't you?" She was surprised at his intentness as he listened to her answer.

"I love it. I shall never really be able to give it up entirely."

At that moment Mae Devlin came in with a pot of fresh coffee. "May I join you two? I wanted to tell you, Lorna, how much I enjoyed the play. The girls did a beautiful job." She filled their cups. "Judy's performance impressed me most of all. I'll confess now that when she first arrived, I was afraid she was going to need more help than we could give her. But you've worked hard with her and I think everything will be all right."

"You didn't tell me you doubted."

Mae smiled. "I couldn't suggest any better procedure myself. You were spending at least one hour every day with her. When you can't improve on something, I've found that silence is the best policy."

Greg put down his cup. "We were just starting to discuss Judy's schooling," he told Mae. "I'd appreciate hearing your opinion on the matter." The three of them talked at some length, and it was finally agreed that Judy would start her nurse's aid training after the holidays.

Then Greg asked Mae a question about her early days in social work, and she began to relate some of her experiences. It was fascinating to hear how the field had developed, and they speculated broadly on the possibilities for the future.

"It's young people like you who will determine the importance of social work in years to come," Mae told them, drawing the conversation to a close.

The library clock began to chime. "Midnight so soon?" Lorna exclaimed. "I had no idea it was so late. This has been one of the nicest evenings I've had in—in a long time."

Greg's eyes flickered briefly over her face. "The same goes for me," he said. "We'll have to do it again soon."

Mae chuckled a bit as she rose. "These late hours may be fine for you youngsters, but not for me. I've really enjoyed it though."

"May I give either or both of you ladies a lift home?" Greg inquired as he helped them with their coats.

"Thanks," Mae told him, "but I have my car."

"Me too," Lorna added, and found herself wishing that she had taken a bus back to the Y. Greg's presence was somehow relaxing, comforting . . .

She waved good-by and got into her Volkswagen, thinking how nice everyone had been about her broken engagement. No one had asked a single question, even though the absence of the diamond ring was conspicuous. Her customary buoyancy and enthusiasm had failed her these last two weeks, but her friends and co-workers had been careful not to comment on the noticeable change in her spirits. "From now on," she told herself, "I must do better. I've made my decision and I must live with it, no matter how much it hurts. In time, I'll get over it. . . . Please, God, make it soon . . ."

Chapter Ten

Because the play and additional counseling had required so much of her time, Lorna had to postpone her interview with Lily Ricardo's sister. Mrs. Hart had been so disappointed that Lorna called the girl in for two "informal" chats but had learned nothing new. Lily still clung to the original version of her story. Her manner was slightly belligerent, which bothered Lorna, but otherwise the girl seemed to be adjusting nicely to her new surroundings.

On the Tuesday following the play, Lorna was in the middle of a letter to Glennie, who was writing her almost every week, when the telephone interrupted her. It was Mrs. Whitney.

"Miss Evans, I have a call for you on another line—it's someone from the Police Department. I thought I'd let you know before connecting you. Do you want to take it now?"

"Of course. I expect it's just some routine inquiry." Or possibly Pete Huston, although she could think of no reason why he should be calling her. Maybe he wanted her to give a message to Nola . . .

"Is this Miss Evans?" The masculine voice at the other end of the line was definitely not Pete's.

"Yes. May I help you?"

"I hope so. We have two girls down here at the station who say they live at the Y. Lily Ricardo and Jennifer Lawrence—do you know them? They gave me your name."

"I know them and they do live here. But I'm afraid I don't understand. Are you *holding* them there?"

"Yes, ma'am, we are. They were picked up for shoplifting, along with two other girls."

"*Shoplifting?*" Lorna realized that she was not sounding very professional at the moment, and tried to assume a calmer tone. "I gather that you have definite proof——" She listened for several minutes while the man explained the circumstances further, then she asked, "May I see them if I come down?"

"Yes, ma'am. I suggest that you do so as soon as you can; one of them seems pretty upset."

I'll bet I know which one, Lorna thought as she hung up. After debating with herself a few moments she decided not to inform Mrs. Hart yet, but she thought it advisable to consult with Mae Devlin before going to the jail, where she was told the girls would be held. Unfortunately, the Executive Director was attending a meeting at another welfare agency, so Lorna had no choice but to proceed on her own.

"The call was nothing urgent," she said in answer to Mrs. Whitney's inquiring look. "I'll be out for a while; please take any messages that come in for me."

The jail was on one of the upper floors of the new County City Building; Lorna had never been there before. She asked the matron if there was a small conference chamber available where she could speak with the two girls more privately than the large, open visitors' room permitted; and the matron led her to a side office.

A few minutes later the door opened and Lorna was distressed at the sight of the two pathetic-looking figures that entered. Lily could easily have been mistaken for a child—a lost child. The skirt and sweater she was wearing only accentuated her thinness; all signs of defiance were gone. Jennifer was so pale that Lorna thought she was about to faint. Her eyes were red-rimmed from hours of weeping.

Lily was the first to speak. "Oh Miss Evans, thank heavens you've come! This is just terrible! I've never done anything like this before, honest! It wasn't my fault. Those other girls are to blame——"

"What other girls, Lily?" Lorna cut in. "Who are they?"

"Two kids I know—Minnie and Gladys. They said they got their nice things from the stores. Jen and I went with them today, but I didn't really mean to *steal* anything . . ."

"And what about you, Jennifer?" Lorna asked.

The girl shook her head, tears beginning to stream down her cheeks. "I'm—so—sorry—" she sobbed.

Lorna turned back to Lily: "Why did you take her with you?" No answer. "Did she take anything?" Still no word from Lily, but she began to look sullen.

"I didn't take a thing, Miss Evans," Jennifer managed to sob out.

"Well, Lily, haven't you anything more to say?" Lorna was not feeling very sympathetic toward the girl at the moment.

"I only took a sweater. Minnie stole some jewelry and Gladys stole gloves, a scarf, and a real fancy beaded sweater. I didn't see if Jen took anything."

"You know perfectly well I didn't! I told you I wouldn't and I told *you* not to!" Jennifer protested.

"All right, Jennifer, calm down now. Did you tell the police this?" Lorna asked.

"Yes, but I don't think they believed me, even though they didn't find anything when they searched me."

Lorna felt sure she was telling the truth. Why, then, didn't the police believe her? "Lily," she said sternly, "you admitted stealing the sweater, but you didn't tell the police that Jennifer was innocent. Why not?"

Lily's eyes showed fear, but she was otherwise unruffled. She met Lorna's look defiantly. "What was the use to lie about the sweater? They found it under my coat. But I can only speak for myself—I wasn't watching Jen every minute."

"That's a very mean way to behave, Lily. You *know* Jennifer didn't steal anything! Have you no sense of loyalty to your friend?"

The girl opened her eyes wide, staring blankly at Lorna. Obviously the thought had never occurred to her.

The conversation seemed to be getting nowhere, so Lorna told them that she would notify their families and then make whatever other arrangements were necessary. Jennifer grew hysterical, pleading with her not to tell her parents, but Lorna made it clear that under the circumstances she had no choice but to inform them. Lily was indifferent, claiming that her sister and brother-in-law would not care what happened to her.

Lorna got up. "I think you are wrong about them, Lily, but we shall soon find out. I'm going over to see them."

At that the girl jumped to her feet. "Don't do that! They'll only say bad things about me."

"If what they say is untrue, you don't have anything to worry about," Lorna replied coolly.

Jennifer dried her eyes. "Miss Evans, please help me. I know that it was wrong of me to go with them, even if I didn't steal anything. I'm so afraid . . . what will they do to me . . . ?"

Lorna could not answer that question but tried to reassure both girls that she would do the best she could to help them. As soon as she left the jail, she went straight to Peter Huston's office in the Youth Guidance Department and told him what had happened.

"I'm sure Jennifer Lawrence is innocent," she added. "But I feel guilty about Lily Ricardo because I should have investigated her background before accepting her at the Residence and I didn't."

"Well, we all make mistakes," Pete said. "And Lily looks deceptively innocent. However, this is not the first time she's been held in custody." He went on to explain that she had been picked up about two years ago in a teen-age fight. She was released when her sister pleaded to have her sent back home instead of to a reformatory.

Lorna was incredulous. "What happens now?" she asked worriedly.

"There'll be a hearing tomorrow. But don't get yourself upset. The court is never too hard on kids. Just remember one thing—Lily is eighteen now and shoplifting isn't kids' play."

Lorna found small comfort in this.

The first thing she did when she got back to her office was telephone the girls' families. The Lawrences lived in Franklin, a small town twenty miles away. The mother was so distraught that she was unable to do anything but leave the matter entirely in Lorna's hands until after the court hearing. After that, she said, Mr. Lawrence would take over, and do whatever the judge deemed best. The conversation was very painful for Lorna and it took her a few minutes to compose herself before calling Lily's sister, Tina.

She explained briefly what had happened, adding that she

thought it best to talk things over in person. Tina said that her husband Albert would be home at five-thirty, and asked Lorna to come over around six.

Next, Lorna called Mae's office, only to learn that she would not be returning to the Y that day. After making out a detailed report, Lorna asked Mrs. Hart to drop by her office. Deeply embarrassed, she recounted the afternoon's events, ending with an apology for not having followed up the case promptly. "All this might have been avoided," she said unhappily.

The Housemother was very tactful, pointing out that no one could have predicted this trouble. "What I regret most is Jennifer's involvement in all of this. She had a nice job with a paper company here in Tacoma and was doing so well. She's a good girl."

A few minutes later Mrs. Hart left and Lorna put through a call to Greg Taylor. "I hope I'm not interrupting you," she said.

"Not at all," he assured her. "You sound upset, Lorna. Is it anything serious?" He listened attentively as she told him about Lily and Jennifer. "Stop blaming yourself," he told her gently when she finished. "I'm going to be in court tomorrow anyway; why don't you meet me for lunch before the girls' case comes up before the judge. We can talk further about this thing and see what can be worked out for those two kids."

"That's very kind of you, Greg; I'd like that very much."

"Fine. Then I'll pick you up at twelve-thirty," he replied. "And stop worrying, Lorna. Everything will be okay."

On her way out to see Lily's sister a short while later, Lorna reflected on Greg's sympathetic response to the situation. "Why, oh why couldn't Farley have been like that?" she asked herself, feeling a dull ache begin to throb within her as memories flooded back. She tried very hard to control her mind, but there were times when it was impossible to shut out the image of Farley's face, the sound of his voice. In time she would forget; meanwhile she must keep busy and try not to think, remember . . .

Suddenly she realized that she had reached an unfamiliar part of the city and she peered anxiously at the poorly lighted signposts at each intersection, wondering if she could find her way through the maze of dark, narrow streets. Just as she was about to admit that she was lost, she spotted a paint-chipped sign on which she could barely make out the name she was looking for. Halfway down the block she found the house, run-down and sadly in need of paint. Sighing with relief, she parked the car, locking it as an afterthought.

The woman who opened the door in response to the doorbell was as small as Lily, but older and very tired-looking. Lorna followed her into a shabby but clean dining room, and they sat down facing one another across a small table.

"Miss Evans, I'm sorry you got involved in this mess," Tina began, her eyes meeting Lorna's steadily. Her simple dignity in the midst of privation and trouble was touching. "We have tried our best with Lily, but she is so impulsive—not a bad girl, mind you—she won't listen to me or Albert when we try to help her . . ." Her velvet black eyes filled with tears and she moved her hands helplessly.

Lorna was explaining the problem that now faced Lily when Tina's husband entered the room. His gruffness poorly concealed the fact that he was deeply worried. After asking his wife to serve them some coffee, he turned to Lorna and spoke urgently:

"I don't want Tina to be more upset than she already is, you understand. I don't make much money, but I tried to give Lily a good home. We've been kind to her, but she's ungrateful, that one, and wild. All we asked her to do was baby-sit once in a while so Tina could get out for a few hours. And what would Lily do? She'd have boys and girls in, play the radio loud, wake up the babies and make the neighbors complain, drink *vino* and sass me back when I came home and told her to behave herself——" He broke off as Tina came in with a tray.

There was silence as she filled the three coffee cups and offered her visitor some cookies.

"Lily is young, Albert," Tina said, gazing at her husband with sad eyes. "She meant no harm."

"Maybe, but she always chooses bad companions and won't listen to anyone who wants to help her," he replied, restraining the anger for the sake of his wife. "We didn't want her to leave here, Miss Evans, but we couldn't stop her."

Lorna sighed as she stirred her coffee. "I'm afraid that I should have come to see you much, much sooner. If I had, perhaps, all this could have been avoided . . ."

Tina reached out a timid hand. "Oh no, don't think that. Lily has a way of getting around people, and I would not have admitted to you before that she has been a heartache to us. "Now," she raised her shoulders eloquently, "we cannot hide the truth."

"There will be a hearing tomorrow, and I shall be there to do whatever I can to help, although I can promise nothing," Lorna told them. "If the court should decide to give Lily another chance, would you accept responsibility for her and have her live with you again?"

Tina and Albert looked at each other. "I don't know," he said doubtfully. "It would depend on how she would behave if we did."

"We want to help," Tina whispered. "But we don't know what is best for her and us. You understand, don't you?"

Lorna nodded. "I think you're being wise to think it over before making any decision. It won't be necessary for you to appear tomorrow, if you authorize me to speak in your behalf. I shall ask the judge for some time to discuss the situation further with you, and I'll call you in the afternoon as soon as I can."

Tina broke into tears and begged Lorna to take her to the courthouse for Lily's hearing. Albert put his arms gently around his wife and nodded to Lorna.

"It's all right, Miss Evans, she's upset now, but I won't let her go tomorrow. We trust you and know you'll do everything you can for Lily."

Lorna assured him that she would. Bidding them good night, she hurried back to her car. The emotional strain of the interview had exhausted and depressed her. It was too late to reproach herself any more about Lily, but she vowed that in the future she would follow up all the routine details of her job—even if they seemed unnecessary—and listen to the opinions and warnings of more experienced people like Mrs. Hart.

Greg Taylor arrived a few minutes after twelve-thirty and told Lorna that he knew a wonderful little restaurant near the courthouse, where they could enjoy lunch and conversation without any crowds or last-minute rush.

"There's not much we can do for the two girls before we hear the court's verdict. Therefore I have a suggestion: I promise not to discuss business, if you will promise the same," he said as he opened the car door for her.

She agreed, and both kept their word, except for a brief mention of Judy Stillman's continuing progress. Over lunch he told her about the job he had had before joining the Tacoma Child Guidance Bureau. Many of the views he expressed about social work were ones that Lorna shared, and as the conversation extended to other subjects, she found that they had many interests in common. Being with Greg was both comfortable and refreshing, she thought as they left the restaurant.

However, her nervousness returned as they entered the courtroom, and it did not help to have to sit through two other hearings that preceded the one she had come for. Her attention wandered during the long-drawn-out proceedings, and glancing about, she spotted Lily's brother-in-law a few rows ahead of her. When the clerk announced the names of the four girls as they were led into the court, Albert turned around and gave Lorna a reassuring nod. Apparently, he and Tina had decided to take Lily back, if the judge ruled in her favor.

Jennifer was very pale and her eyes still showed traces of weeping. After one quick glance around the room, she kept her gaze fixed on the judge. Lily appeared remarkably calm, under the circumstances, although she flushed when she saw Albert. She smiled hesitantly at Lorna, then turned her head so that she could not see the spectators.

Lorna inspected the other two girls curiously. She had never seen them before.

Minnie was tall, rather attractive, but with an aggressive air about her as she stood ignoring everyone in the crowded room, including the judge. Gladys, on the other hand, was small and slender, with a profusion of hair as blonde as Minnie's was dark. She seemed nervous, stealing occasional side glances at the audience all through the hearings.

After the charge was read the judge asked each girl, "How do you plead?"

The response "Guilty" came from all but Jennifer, who replied, "Not guilty, your Honor."

The judge studied her intently. "In that case I must postpone your hearing until"—he consulted the calendar—"December Thirtieth. Bail is set at one hundred dollars." He waited until Jennifer was led back into the anteroom, then turned a stern face to the remaining three.

"Shoplifting is a very serious offense," he began, leafing through the case reports before him. "I see that the amount in each case does not exceed fifty dollars. The sentence will be thirty days; however, Lily Ricardo, yours will be suspended since this is your first time." He paused and frowned at the girl. "But I warn you, if you are brought in again on this charge, you will not be let off so easily."

The case was dismissed, but as the three girls were leaving the court, a sound of smothered laughter trickled back to the bench.

"One moment!" the judge called out sharply. "Bring those girls back!" The tone of his voice sent a murmur through the audience. "Were you giggling?" he demanded of Lily, who was suddenly too terrified by his angry expression to do anything but nod yes.

"If you think this court is so funny, I think you'd better spend a week in jail and find out exactly how funny this whole matter is!"

Lily gasped and clenched her hands, but she dared not say a word. Lorna caught sight of the tears that began to roll down her cheeks as she turned away and slowly walked out of the courtroom.

The judge called a recess and Albert hurried over to Lorna, bursting into conversation before she could introduce Greg.

"That Lily! You see how she is? This time she can't get away with it, though. I'm glad Tina isn't here to see this. I hate to break the bad news to her."

It took a few minutes to calm him down, and finally he left, shaking his head.

Greg and Lorna spoke to Jennifer Lawrence's parents, who had managed to get to Tacoma for the hearing. After talking to the city attorney, Mr. Lawrence paid the hundred dollar bail and they hurried away to pick up their daughter and take her back home until December Thirtieth.

"We'll see how things are after Christmas," the mother said before leaving. "If Jennifer wants to, she can remain in Tacoma and work. She's a good girl and we know nothing like this will ever happen again."

"I'm sure it won't," Lorna agreed.

Greg touched her arm. "I was hoping we'd have a few minutes to discuss this whole situation, but I'm afraid I've got to leave," he said. "A client of mine has a case coming up after recess and I must catch him before the hearing starts."

"You've been a great help to me already, Greg, and I'm grateful to you. Just sitting in that courtroom, unable to do anything but listen, is *awful*."

He nodded. "I know exactly what you mean—the first few times it's really rough. I'll get in touch with you in a few days and maybe we can think of some way to help Lily after she is released." Greg paused, looking steadily into Lorna's eyes. "Meanwhile, take care of yourself, young lady, and stop worrying so much. Remember, you can't win 'em all! Are you going home for Christmas? It might do you good to get away for a few days."

Lorna shook her head. "No, I plan to be here. I saw my folks at Thanksgiving and . . . and I'm so busy at the Y, I decided it would be best to stay. Anyway my roommate has no place to go and I thought we could keep each other company. It's terrible to be alone on a holiday like Christmas . . ." Lorna stopped. It was obvious that Greg knew about her breakup with Farley, even though he had very tactfully avoided any mention of it; but she did not want to give the impression of being forlorn and miserable, so she added, "By the way, we're having open house from two to six on Christmas Day, if you care to drop by."

"I'll take you up on that, Lorna. Right now I must run, but let me make one suggestion that doesn't assure victory every time but is a lot easier on the nervous system: tackle the world's problems one at a time . . . Promise?" Smiling gently at her, Greg held her hand for one moment as she nodded mutely, touched by his concern for her. The next moment he was gone.

Chapter Eleven

Fortunately the week preceding Christmas was so hectic, Lorna had little time to brood about Lily's unfortunate predicament. Furthermore, both Mae Devlin and Mrs. Hart had assured her that they did not hold her responsible for what had happened and that they had all learned something from the experience. The Executive Director added that she trusted Lorna to follow up the case in whatever way seemed best for all concerned, and the matter was dropped. Their attitude restored some of Lorna's own confidence, which had been badly shaken by the whole affair.

At the Y, she was caught up in the excitement of last-minute arrangements for Christmas parties, dances, and a Nativity Pageant. She spent her lunch hours searching the department stores and shops for the gifts she had found no time to buy earlier: a soft, fine-knit crimson sweater for Nola that would add a dramatic touch of color to her friend's dark-haired beauty; a book of Debussy piano selections for Judy; and, after careful thought, a soft leather purse for Glennie, *"For the day, soon to come, when you return to Tacoma."*

During the staff Christmas party, Lorna received a call from Gregory Taylor, who said that he had heard about a job he thought Lily Ricardo would probably be able to get, if she was willing to work. Lorna told him that she had discussed the situation thoroughly with Tina and Albert and that Lily herself seemed chastened by her experience and had agreed to come in for weekly counseling.

"I'll tell you more about the job when I see you after the holiday. It sounds like a good opportunity, provided Lily can take *proper* advantage of it," Greg said. "If she's interested, I'll talk to her, then send her to see the personnel man who told me about the job. We can but try, Lorna. Well, I won't keep you any longer. I can hear noises in the background— sounds like an office party. Have fun, and I'll see you around three Christmas Day."

Lorna felt a warm glow surge through her as she rejoined her co-workers. Greg certainly went all out to help people.

The staff had been invited to the Residence "Christmas Sing," to be held shortly after the office party. As Lorna and Bea entered the large recreation room where it was being given, their eyes were caught by the large, softly lighted tree at the far end of the darkened room. Sally Williams, Lenore Coleman and two other girls formed a welcoming committee and led guests to the comfortable chairs that had been arranged in a loose semi-circle in front of the tree. As soon as the program began, it was clear that the girls had practiced long and hard. The carols were beautifully sung, and Judy was at the piano, accompanying the group. It gave Lorna a deep sense of satisfaction to see that she was no longer the trembling, terrified girl who had tried to shut out the world. Judy played two solo Christmas songs with great tenderness and feeling, and smiled in quiet pleasure at the enthusiastic applause from both the audience and the choral singers.

When the musical program was over, the lights were turned up and the guests invited to enjoy the refreshments laid out at the other end of the room. Mae Devlin looked around in amazement and asked who had done such a stunning job of decorating the room. Everyone on the staff was admiring the red, green, and gold color design and arrangement which showed considerable ingenuity in planning and execution.

Lorna heard one of the girls say, "Isn't it terrific? Mabel Parsons, who was chairman of the decorating committee, asked Grace Walker if she'd be willing to help. Well, as it turned out, Grace had some great ideas and she and Mabel really did all the 'creative' work. The rest of us just carried out orders of how and where to put things. Golly, it was some job, but it was worth it!"

Mrs. Hart caught Lorna's eye, gave a secret smile and Lorna nodded happily as she headed toward Grace and Mabel, who were beaming at the compliments and praise everyone was expressing. Another beginning had been made.

That night, when Nola and Lorna finished hanging the last ornament on their plump little tree, they turned off some of the lamps and for a few minutes sat admiring it. The tree shimmered and glittered as the winking lights caught the silvery tinsel strands and fragile ornaments in their brief on-and-off glow. Then the girls went into the kitchen to attend to last-minute menu preparations for the next day.

"What were those packages you brought in this evening? Presents from the Y?" Nola asked as they opened olives, pickles, and began cracking walnuts.

Lorna nodded. "A few of us exchanged little gifts and one or two of the girls handed me packages as I was leaving. It was sweet of them, but I felt rather embarrassed. I could hardly give all of them presents, you know."

"You've been giving them something all along, Lorna—

your trust, your help, many hours of your time. This is their way of saying Thanks."

"I suppose you're right." Lorna smiled gently. "By the way, a package from Glennie arrived at the office this morning. I can't imagine what it could be."

"You'll find out tomorrow, pet. No cheating tonight by opening *anything*. Okay?"

"Okay."

The last thing they did before going to bed was to arrange the presents under the tree.

"They're too pretty to open," Lorna murmured as she fixed the bow on the box her parents had sent her.

"I doubt you'll feel that way in the morning! Come on, let's get some sleep. We have a busy day ahead of us."

At one-thirty on Christmas Day Nola stood in front of the dressing table mirror, admiring the red sweater from Lorna. "It fits perfectly and feels positively yummy," she said. "How did you know I wanted one just this color?"

"That's my secret," Lorna told her with an air of mystery. "And how did you find out that my folks were sending me this blue dress? You've matched the color perfectly in this pin and earring set. They look heavenly with it."

"Oh, it was easy," Nola said with an airy wave of her hand. "I just looked into my crystal ball and there it was. Heavens! There's the doorbell, our first guests have arrived."

She rushed out of the bedroom and Lorna could hear her greeting the arrivals. Pete's deep voice boomed out "Merry Christmas!" in admirable imitation of St. Nick, and the echoing phrases told her that others had arrived with him.

After a final dab of perfume behind her ears, Lorna entered the living room, with barely time to say hello before the doorbell rang again. After that, there seemed to be a steady

146 •

parade from the front door to the punch bowl to fill cups with rich, creamy eggnog, to the kitchen for more sandwiches or "nibbles," and every time she walked through the living room there seemed to be more people.

She had just returned from putting some coats in the bedroom and was reaching for her barely tasted eggnog when a quiet voice behind her said, "A very Merry Christmas, Lorna." She turned to meet Gregory Taylor's nice gray eyes.

"And to you too, Greg," she said softly, giving him her free hand. "I'm glad you came."

"Me too. It's a lovely party," he told her, looking around at the many familiar faces. Most of the people were those who were in one or another phase of social work, plus others they had met through their professional contacts. "Here, let me unburden this on you. I don't know where you want to put it; the place is so beautifully decorated already."

He handed her a delicately flowering potted plant, which she had to use both hands to accept. He held her cup while she cleared a space on the buffet table for it.

"This is just the spot for it, Greg. Everyone will be able to enjoy it if we put it here for now. How thoughtful of you to bring it."

"My pleasure," he said in a gentle voice, gazing at her intently for a moment. "Here's your cup; I'll fill mine and we'll drink to the New Year." His cup touched hers and they smiled at each other before sipping. "You look lovely, Lorna; blue becomes you."

Her mingled embarrassment and pleasure at his sincere compliment made her blush. No one since Farley had said anything like this to her and she became acutely aware of this man's presence, his gentleness, his consideration for her as a person. She had not had much time to think about Farley lately, but suddenly she remembered—oh, so many things—and wondered what he was doing this Christmas Day, which they had planned to spend together.

"Do you know everyone here?" she asked huskily, trying to hide the surge of mixed emotions that filled her.

"I think so. In any case, I'll soon find out. I see a few friends over there—is that Dr. Marlow? I'll go over and say hello, in order not to monopolize the attention of the hostess." There was understanding in his expression as he looked at her once more, before leaving to join a group.

Lorna had little chance to talk with Greg since guests came and went, but his observant eye missed nothing and several times he helped her to bring things in and out of the kitchen and pass trays of food among the small clusters of people who filled the room. Little by little the guests left, each one telling Lorna and Nola how enjoyable this Christmas Open House had been.

As Lorna was heading for the bedroom to get some coats, Greg stopped her. "I don't mean to intrude, but I'm a whiz at dishwashing, if you're willing to have an extra pair of hands around. May I help?"

Lorna was genuinely surprised at his offer. "Why, that's very generous of you, Greg, but it's hardly a way to spend part of your holiday! Surely your family or some friends have something planned——"

"Don't worry about that. I'd like to stay, if you and Nola are not rushing off somewhere yourselves. I have to leave around eight-thirty, but otherwise I have nothing I must, or want, to do."

"In that case, you're hired." Lorna laughed. "Pete is going to stay too—he claims he's an ideal busboy. With four of us working, we should be finished in record time. Then we can take our shoes off and relax. Believe me, Nola and I will be too tired to go *anywhere* else tonight."

In less than an hour they had things washed and put away and were all back in the living room, sipping fresh coffee and nibbling on Nola's cookies. The conversation wandered into amiable, relaxed channels until Greg glanced at his watch. To everyone's surprise, it was almost nine o'clock and both men rose to leave.

"Goodnight, Nola, Lorna," Greg said. "This has been a very happy Christmas for me, and I can thank you both for helping to make it so—perhaps more than you realize."

"I wonder what he meant by that?" Lorna mused, leaning back against the door when it closed behind him.

Nola smiled. "Who knows? . . . Greg Taylor is quite a guy, really an unusually nice person." She kicked off her shoes and yawned. "He seems fond of you, pet." She regarded her friend speculatively. "What do you think?"

"Me? I don't think anything." Lorna yawned too. "I hope he likes me. I certainly like him and want him as a friend. I respect many things about him and trust his judgment and opinions more than almost anyone else I can think of. Funny I should feel that way—knowing him so short a time."

"What's time got to do with it? He inspires confidence, because he's so thoughtful and considerate in everything he says and does. I, for one, hope we see more of him."

"So do I," Lorna said, then added, irrelevantly, "He dates Marianne, you know."

"So what? That proves nothing—at least not as far as Greg Taylor is concerned."

The two friends fell silent, each absorbed in her own thoughts for some time. Finally Lorna got up and turned out the tree lights.

"Glennie's gift was sweet," she murmured, picking up a box containing a set of checkers and a board. She reread the note:

Dear Miss Evans: I think I'm learning how to make moves and not lose so many men. I still remember what you said about having a better chance to win the game that way. I know you were right. Merry Christmas.

                                              Love, Glennie

PS. Thank you for my beautiful present. I haven't opened it yet but I know I'll love it, whatever it is, because it's from you.

Tears filled Lorna's eyes. No one—not Farley Knowles, not anybody—would ever convince her that a human being's future happiness, maybe a whole future life, was not worth a gamble.

Chapter Twelve

The holiday spirit still pervaded the Y.W.C.A., making it difficult for Lorna to settle down to work. But she could not afford to idle away the time; there were too many details to attend to. She checked on the arrangements for the Golden Age Club dance the following evening, contacted Mary Renlo about a painting exhibit that had been proposed, and made several follow-up appointments with some Residence girls she had seen earlier in the month. After looking over the January schedule of events and making some necessary changes, she answered her mail and then turned to a stack of folders on her desk that needed to be brought up to date. As she was entering her comments and suggestions in them, a light tap on her door made her look up. Judy Stillman was standing in the open doorway with some booklets under her arm.

"I just wanted to thank you for the lovely Debussy you gave me," the young girl said rather breathlessly as Lorna beckoned her in. "How did you know he was one of my very favorites?" Her eyes lighted up as she caught sight of the handkerchief that peeped out of the pocket of Lorna's tailored wool dress. "Do you like them?" she asked shyly, referring to the three embroidered and initialed hankies she had made for Lorna.

"They're beautiful, Judy—I could never buy anything as lovely."

They chatted while Lorna looked over the school brochures that Judy had brought with her. The girl was excited at the prospect of beginning her course so soon, and said she could hardly wait till classes started.

"I'm on my way down to the school now," she announced happily, "to meet with my adviser and plan my program for the first term. Isn't it wonderful?" she asked as she got up to leave.

"It certainly is," Lorna agreed, walking with her to the door.

"You'd never think that was the same girl who came in here just a couple of months ago, would you?" Bea said, stepping into Lorna's office a few seconds after Judy had left.

"I was thinking exactly the same thing. It's this kind of a result that makes all the disappointments and frustrations in social work worthwhile."

Bea nodded, smiling. "I just thought I'd tell you that I'll be glad to answer your phone while you're at the staff meeting this afternoon."

Lorna gave a little whistle. "It's a good thing you reminded me—I'd completely forgotten about it. I wonder what it's being held for; this isn't one of the scheduled meetings."

She was soon to find out, and the knowledge did not make her very happy. As soon as the staff members had arrived, Mae Devlin closed her door and made the opening statement:

"I'm afraid my news is not too good. The United Good Neighbor funds are considerably below last year's, which unfortunately means that all of the agencies will suffer a cut in their budgets." She went on to discuss the consequences this would have on the Y staff, which would have to be reduced. In turn she spoke to each member, pointing out where changes would have to be made in order to reapportion the workload.

"I'm very sorry, Lorna," Mae said, "but I'm afraid we'll have to let Bea go. I'll take over the counseling again—even though you're doing an excellent job—and you'll have to assume responsibility for group work again. I hate to have to do this, but there's no other way to handle the situation."

Lorna returned to her office after the meeting and stared glumly out the window. She hated to see Bea dropped, because she needed the job and had proved to be extremely competent in managing the group work, which she loved doing. As for herself, she now realized that counseling was really what she wanted to do, and she was reluctant to give it up. But was there any alternative if she intended to remain at the Y?

Suddenly she remembered her conversation with Grace Heaton of the Family Service Agency . . . "If you ever consider making a change, come and see me" . . . Perhaps *that* was the answer! Of course there might not be an opening at F.S.A. at present, but there was no point in delaying a call to find out.

"Would Miss Heaton have any time to see me this afternoon?" Lorna asked the Agency switchboard operator.

"Just a moment, please"—there was a short pause—"Miss Heaton says to come over anytime after four, Miss Evans."

At four-fifteen Lorna went downstairs, feeling a sharp sense of regret at the possibility of leaving this place, where she had been so happy; but she had to make a change if she hoped to pursue a career in case work. As she walked the few blocks to the Family Service Agency, she felt a momentary anger because the people of Tacoma had not given the U.G.N. the funds it needed to function more fully. The mood passed, however, when she considered the fact that a recent strike had affected many family incomes, and the cost of living was rising all the time too. Besides, how could people know the desperate need of youngsters like Glennie and Judy unless they actually had met such girls? How could they know that even the smallest contribution might make the vital difference between hope and despair, a promising future or a wrecked life?

Grace Heaton was forthright and easy to talk to. Lorna had the impression that a person would always know where he or she stood with Grace.

"You couldn't have come at a more opportune time," she said as soon as she learned the reason for Lorna's visit. "We received some private funds a short while ago and have been looking for another social worker to add to our staff. So far we've seen no one we wanted to hire, but I know your qualifications and I think you'd fit in perfectly. We'd be very happy to have you join us, if you've definitely decided to leave the Y."

Such luck seemed almost too good to be true. "You realize, of course, that I have not had a great deal of experience in case work," Lorna said, not wanting to misrepresent the situation.

"Don't let that bother you; we all help one another here, no matter how much experience any of us has had. Furthermore, Mae Devlin has spoken very highly of you and the job you've done at the Y. Anyone who has worked for Mae has had excellent training, so we are not concerned about the fact that you did counseling at the Y for only a few months. In any case, there's always a lot to learn in every new job." Grace paused to answer her phone, then continued. "Does Mae know you're planning to leave?"

"No," Lorna replied. "I wanted to talk to you before saying anything. Naturally I'll have to discuss it with Miss Devlin before accepting this job, but I'm certain that Bea Miller will be able to take my place in group work."

"Well, I'll call Mae tomorrow afternoon, after you've had a chance to talk things over with her. How soon would you be able to join the staff here, Lorna?"

"In about two weeks, I think."

"Fine. I very much hope you decide to come with us." Her parting handshake was hearty and firm.

At nine-fifteen the next morning Lorna went in to see Mae Devlin. She explained that she would not have considered leaving the Y if it had not been necessary to cut the staff. But, she confessed frankly, case work was far more interesting than group work and she did not want to pass up the opportunity with the Family Service Agency, if Mae felt that Bea could handle the workload.

The Executive Director nodded firmly. "Of course she can. I wouldn't dream of standing in your way, Lorna; this *is* an excellent chance for you to broaden your experience and I know you'll be happy working with Grace Heaton." Mae studied Lorna closely. "I'm sure you're not making the change just so Bea can stay on. It's a wise decision on your part, my dear, for you have shown unusual capability in counseling. We'll be very sorry to lose you, but I think it's best for you."

Bea cried when she heard what had happened. "I'm so happy for you, as well as for myself," she told Lorna. "I had heard about a staff cut and I was sure I'd be the one to go.

I know you didn't leave just because of me—but I'm sure that had something to do with your decision."

Lorna assured her that the major factor was her desire to continue counseling. "But I also know what a terrific job you've done here, Bea, and it only seemed fair to both of us if I found another job," she added. "Before I leave, we'll spend some time together, looking over the projects that have been suggested or planned. But there's very little that you don't know about this job already."

That afternoon Greg Taylor called. "Are you free around five, Lorna? My schedule is jammed, but I want to see you today, about Lily Ricardo primarily, because my contact would have to see her tomorrow. He can't delay any longer."

"Well . . . it's a little awkward, Greg; there's a dance here tonight that I'm to chaperone—but I could see you around seven, if you could arrange to meet me here before it starts. I do have to go home and change first." Lorna had an unaccountable desire to see him again and she was delighted to hear him say, "That's fine with me. Why don't I pick you up at your place around six-thirty, and we can dine somewhere in town, then I'll drop you off at the Y in time for your dance. I wanted to talk to you about Judy too, so we'll need a couple of hours. I was going to ask you to join me for dinner anyway. It's much nicer to talk in a restaurant than an office. That way it doesn't seem so much like work!"

Lorna laughed. "On the contrary, it's a pleasure. I'll see you at six-thirty."

When Greg arrived, Lorna suggested a restaurant that was not too far from the Y. Greg was interested to hear about the Family Service Agency job, so Lorna told him what she knew about it. "Of course there's a lot I still have to learn about it myself," she added, "but I love case work—which is the most important thing."

Over dinner they discussed Lily's future. The girl had returned to her sister's home and wanted to try out for the job Greg had in mind. Lorna mentioned that Tina and Albert were going to F.S.A. for help in handling Lily, so she would be able to keep informed of the girl's progress.

"I hope she can make it this time," she said. "This may be just the thing to set her on the right road. It was very kind of you to take an interest in her case, Greg."

"We have to help one another," he replied, his gray eyes resting thoughtfully on her face. "Jennifer will be all right, I'm sure, and if she stays on in Tacoma, we'll keep an eye on her."

We, Lorna thought. How considerate he is! I'm lucky to have him as a friend as well as a fellow social worker. But she did not voice these thoughts and Greg passed on to Judy's case, which they finished discussing by the time dessert came.

"I'm afraid I have to run soon," Lorna said apologetically, glancing at her watch. "The dance starts at eight-thirty, but I want to check up on the refreshments and decorations. This is a Golden Age Club affair and I want everything to be especially nice for the occasion."

"I've heard about that Club—I'm sure they're a wonderful group."

"You wouldn't believe how spirited they are and what fun they have. I wouldn't miss this last meeting with them for anything!" Lorna told him.

Greg finished his coffee and waved to the waiter for the check. "Are party crashers allowed? I wouldn't mind seeing them in action, if it's okay with you."

"I'd love to have you come! Why, I would never have thought you'd be interested, because——" Lorna almost blurted out that Farley had refused to attend the dance but she caught herself in time.

Although Greg did not ask her to finish the sentence, he looked quizzically at her and she had the feeling that he had guessed what she had been about to say.

The Golden Age Dance turned out to be far more fun than Lorna had expected it to be. As the music began for the first dance, Greg led Lorna onto the floor, where they were soon joined by more and more couples. All of them nodded and smiled approvingly at the young couple, and as soon as the first dance ended, a distinguished-looking man who must have been in his eighties, Lorna decided, asked her for the next one. His slight stiffness barely interfered with the gracefulness of his dancing and she received a wonderful courtly bow when the music stopped. Before the evening was over, she had danced with almost every man in the club, and each one responded gallantly to her youthfulness and charm. Greg, meanwhile, was equally popular among the ladies. He helped them mix the punch; he chatted easily with the elderly ones who declined to dance; he waltzed and twirled the sprightly ones around the floor, appearing to be enjoying every minute of it. When Lorna told him this later, he assured her that he had indeed enjoyed the whole affair, and admired the club members for their hearty participation in it.

"If your feet hurt as much as mine," he told her as they danced the last dance together, "how about giving them a rest at the Towers? We can have a cup of coffee before I take you home."

After bidding the last happy guest good night, she checked with the hostess committee in the kitchen and was then ready to leave. "That coffee idea sounds wonderful," she sighed, sinking into the leather-upholstered front seat of Greg's car.

They drove along in comfortable silence for a few minutes, then Greg began to talk quietly.

"I'm very glad I saw the Golden Age Club in action; it's a worthwhile activity for those elderly people. The problem of our aging population is becoming one of the major concerns of our society, now that the average life span has risen to seventy years. There are *fifteen* million people over sixty now; imagine what it will be like in, say, 1975, when there will be *sixty* million! We'll need more organizations like the Golden Age Club, to make those older people as loved, needed, thought of, as the rest of the population. Their pleasure, problems, and need to be useful do not stop just because they reach a certain age."

"You're so right, Greg," Lorna agreed. "Financial assistance or old-age homes are not the whole answer, by any means. People who have been active all their lives cannot suddenly be cut off from all mental stimulation and physical activity without being affected by such a drastic change. To have to sit around doing nothing, feeling discarded by family, friends, and business associates, is the worst possible fate for anyone who still has health and a certain amount of vigor."

"There is a delicate balance between doing enough to help and doing too much," Greg replied, "but then this is true about life in general. Sometimes the decision to help people—whether they do or don't need or want it—robs them of self-respect and incentive. I see this happen often in the case of children."

They had arrived at the Towers, and Greg continued the conversation once they were inside. "I was an orphan, as perhaps you know. I've been very fortunate . . . but there was a time, years ago, when I knew what it was like to feel insecure, unwanted . . . When I grew older, I was determined to help children in some way. The Child Guidance program seemed to provide the best way, and I've never once regretted my decision."

Lorna could not imagine Greg as an unwanted or unloved child; nothing in his quiet, assured manner gave any hint of it. "Tell me about your interests," she urged. "You've never really told me what they are."

"I'm interested in helping disturbed children in particular," he replied. "I feel that it's important to get the children early, before their problems become too acute. For instance I worked with a boy recently whose problem would have been simpler to solve if Joey had been brought to us sooner." He told her more about the youngster, whose mother had not allowed him to grow up. Then he discussed a number of other children, some with whom he felt he had succeeded, some with whom he had failed. Finally he smiled at Lorna. "You're a patient listener, but I don't want to bore you. I get carried away on the subject."

"I'm far from bored," she told him earnestly. "Please go on."

"I have an idea I've been wanting to try. There are quite a few disturbed children who I feel are ready for group experience, and I'd like to organize a camp for them this summer. For two weeks they could be observed during the planned activities that would be supervised by social workers and trained directors. In this way the children would have a chance to test themselves in group situations . . ." He set his coffee cup down and looked at Lorna with a wistful smile. "Quite a dream, isn't it?"

"I think it's wonderful! Why can't you do it?" Then she smiled wryly. "Lack of funds, I suppose? This is always the great problem in social work."

"It's the possible lack of qualified staff, rather than money, that bothers me. Some experience with children is desirable, though not necessary; and I think both men and women should be present, to make it a success. But there may not be enough social workers available at that time. For some it would probably mean giving up their vacation time, which is a lot to ask after working hard all year."

"I'd love to do it!" Lorna exclaimed. "I'm not sure if I'm entitled to a vacation this year, since I'm just joining the staff next month. But I might be able to take time off without pay. I'm sure Grace Heaton would agree that your project is valuable enough to let me do it. Anyway, I could ask."

Greg's expression changed from seriousness to one of pleasure. "If you really want to do it, I'd appreciate it. I think you'd be a great asset to the group."

"I can also ask several people I know if they'd be interested. I'm sure Nola would want to; and maybe Pete. There's also Jo Nordy and Bea Miller from the Y."

"You sound so enthusiastic, maybe between us we'll find enough people to have a camp this summer. If it proves successful, we can have it every year, perhaps for longer than just two weeks." As they walked out to the car he added, "I'm glad I discussed this with you. I haven't had too much time to spend drawing up definite plans, but you've given me such a boost that I'm going to start things perking right away. All the arrangements will take time, so the sooner I begin the better."

Lorna looked up at him with twinkling eyes. "We're being very generous with our friends' summer vacations, aren't we? But I know it will work out."

As he dropped her off in front of her apartment house Greg said, "Thanks for the wonderful opportunity to see the Golden Agers in action, and thanks for your offer to help on this camp project. If I may, I'll call you in a day or two to talk out some ideas I have."

"Any time, Greg. I'm all for it and will do everything I

can to help. And thank *you* for helping to make the evening such a success."

When she settled into bed a short while later, Lorna reflected on the difference between Greg and Farley. With Greg, no explanations were necessary; he understood how she felt about people, about her work. He felt as deeply as she did about the need to help others. Even if Farley had agreed to go to the dance, he would have been bored and she would have felt nervous and apologetic. There was no denying the fact that two people could be drawn to each other and yet be unable to communicate. For herself, no relationship was possible if that realm of silent understanding did not exist—not even real friendship. With Greg she had that kind of understanding . . .

The next morning over breakfast Lorna mentioned the children's camp to Nola and was delighted at the interest her friend immediately showed in the idea—and in Lorna's new job.

New Year's Eve was not an easy night for Lorna. She had declined an invitation to Mary Renlo's party because she did not want to run into Farley or Milli or Marianne. She knew that the whole crowd circulated from house to house before going to a gala club dance, which they attended every year.

Pete and Nola insisted that she join them for late dinner downtown, however, even though she did not want to go.

"Intrude?" Pete boomed out, interrupting Lorna before she could finish her sentence. "We *want* you to come along. We won't take no for an answer!"

So she dressed hurriedly and they drove to the restaurant Pete had chosen. The gaudy decorations—balloons, streamers, paper hats and whistles—added to the festive mood of the parties that were already in full swing at some of the tables. Several people they knew waved and called them over, but they paused only a few moments before continuing to their own table.

Lorna had decided that she would go back to the apartment shortly after dinner so that she could escape the midnight hullabaloo, but service was slow and it was eleven-thirty before dessert was served.

"You can't expect to buck your way home through the crowds, Lorna," Pete told her. "It looks as if you'll have to see the New Year in right here—and I, for one, am glad. What would you do all by yourself?"

Lorna's answer was drowned out by the tooting of a horn over her shoulder, so she merely nodded as Nola leaned forward and patted her arm. The noise and laughter grew louder as the large hand of a brilliantly spotlighted clock crept closer to twelve. On the stroke of midnight, music burst forth, whistles blew, and people were singing, kissing one another, and calling out, "Happy New Year!" Pete gave Nola and Lorna a kiss, looking very pleased with himself as he did so.

"This opportunity to embrace two lovely creatures at once may not come again until next year, so I'd better make the most of it," he joked winking broadly at Lorna. The two girls burst into laughter, then all three joined in the merriment.

It was one o'clock before Lorna finally slipped her house key into the lock and entered the welcome silence of the apartment. She had managed to convince her two friends that she preferred not to join them at one of the parties to which they had all been invited. Her weariness was so great that she fell asleep in the big chair in the living room, awakening only when Nola gently shook her shoulder some hours later and coaxed her to go to bed.

"It was fun being with you and Pete," Lorna murmured sleepily as she snuggled further down under the covers. "How was the . . . party . . . ?" But she was sound asleep before her friend could reply.

As Nola was scrambling eggs for brunch—both girls had slept late that day—she said, "By the way, we ran into Greg Taylor at the party last night—too bad you weren't along. He asked about you, and even called here, but I guess you must have been really sound asleep, not to hear the phone ringing."

"Was he alone?" Lorna asked in surprise.

"As far as Pete and I could tell, he was. Frankly I think he prefers the company of the people he's met professionally to that fancy 'money' crowd. He said he was sorry he hadn't known sooner or he would have gotten in touch with you to arrange a foursome for last night. I guess he figured you had made other plans."

Lorna nodded and changed the subject but she was secretly pleased that Greg had wanted to see her. Nola's news gave her morale a big boost, for she had felt a little sorry for herself because she had not had a date for New Year's Eve. With Farley out of the picture, she had been feeling lost and it was comforting to know that Greg liked her enough to seek her company. "I just hope he isn't doing it because he feels sorry for me . . ." she told herself.

Chapter Thirteen

From the first day Lorna joined the Family Service Agency she knew she had made a wise decision. She was nervous that morning, but Grace Heaton and Ellen Mackay, with whom she would work closely, helped to put her at ease. She met the rest of the staff and then spent the morning studying a copy of *Personal Practices*—which thereafter was always close at her hand. After lunch she read through several case histories and discussed them with Grace, who also told her more about the organization.

Family Service was a private agency, supported by United Good Neighbor funds as well as private contributions. Clients paid what they could afford, but those who had little or no money received equal consideration and care. In order to further acquaint Lorna with the type of problems dealt with at F.S.A., Grace assigned her to the Intake Desk the following day, where she would handle whatever cases came in.

Lorna soon learned that the work was in many ways very different from the job at the Y., although all social work had similar features. Many of the cases here involved marriage counseling, and Lorna had to summon all her courage and training to cope with the first ones, when she faced troubled husbands and wives. Grace Heaton kept a close watch on Lorna, and whenever she sensed that the newcomer was having difficulty, she tactfully routed the case to Ellen Mackay, who was older and wiser in such matters.

"We don't expect you to step into marriage counseling on the spot," Grace told Lorna kindly. "You'll have to observe Ellen in action and when you become acclimated to the procedures and the types of problems brought in here, you'll be able to tackle them on your own. In the meantime—easy does it. You'll have enough to do. You'll see."

Lorna certainly did. Sometimes the problems involved an older person living in the home, and sometimes the children, as well. At other times the cases were much like the ones she had counseled at the Y, involving girls. Ann's case was like that.

Probably the reason Grace Heaton had assigned Ann to her was because of her experience with girls of this age. Ann was eighteen and pregnant, and it was nearing the time when she could no longer conceal her condition nor keep her job. She had come to the Family Service for help because of the blind ad the Agency ran in the classified columns of the daily newspaper, offering to help girls in trouble. Lorna studied the folder on Ann and glanced at her wrist watch. The girl was supposed to come in this afternoon for further counseling.

Hers was not an unfamiliar story, Lorna thought, sighing. Her boy friend, Chet, had disappeared, and when Ann had come to the agency, she had not yet told her family about her condition. After her talk with Lorna she had decided to tell them. She wanted to keep the baby and she would need their help to do so. Lynn wondered how much of an uproar this had caused and hoped the girl's parents would be kind and understanding. "A pretty large hope," she murmured under her breath as she placed the folder back on her desk.

But Ann did not return by closing time and Lorna was regretfully gathering up her things when her telephone rang. It was Greg and her heart leaped at the sound of his voice.

"Lorna, I'm glad I caught you still at the office," he said. "I've just returned from a business trip out of town. Could you have dinner with me tonight?"

"Why, yes. I'd love to. Give me time to change?"

"Of course. I'll pick you up at your apartment in—will an hour do?"

"Nicely, thank you."

"See you then."

Her hand lingered on the telephone after she had returned it to its cradle. Then, sweeping up her things, Lorna snatched up her coat and hurried out of her office.

Comfortably settled at the Towers, Lorna listened as Greg unfolded further plans for the camp. "That was the reason for the business trip," he told her.

"What did you do?" she asked. His usually calm gray eyes were sparkling with excitement.

"I located our camp site," he announced triumphantly. "It looks like this . . ." He whipped out a small pad and sketched on it swiftly. "I used to go there when I was a kid . . . See? There's a lake, boats, wonderful grounds, cabins . . . You are still interested, aren't you?" He studied her anxiously.

"Of course! More than ever. And so is Nola. So that's two for your staff."

"Thanks, Lorna. This means a lot to me—"

She saw him gaze beyond her, as if he recognized someone. And then Farley and Milli were standing at their table. It was the first time Lorna had seen him since she broke their engagement and she felt color shooting up into her face. Mechanically she said the right, polite nothings while Milli stared down at her.

"Won't you two join us?" Greg invited, pulling out a chair. But Milli said, "No, thanks, Greg honey. Farley and I have something special to talk over." Her eyes slid over Lorna and she smiled sweetly. "Some other time——" They had gone off, with Milli clinging to Farley's arm.

"Are they going together again?" Lorna asked and felt stupid even as she spoke.

He nodded, not looking at her. "Not regularly, though." Then his nice gray eyes were full upon her. "Don't let it bother you."

"It doesn't," Lorna said automatically, and suddenly realized that it really didn't. She had been startled to see Farley and Milli—but not "bothered." She didn't suppose Greg believed her. He was very busy stirring his coffee. He didn't know that it was she who had broken the engagement—or why.

Greg asked her about her new job and the incident was brushed aside, but as they talked, Lorna began to wonder about Marianne. Was Greg still going with her? He never mentioned her—but then, of course he wouldn't. For all the pleasure their meetings gave her, the reason for them was always business. Greg sought her out only on professional problems.

As if to bear out that thought, Greg said, "Wait till you see the kids I'm lining up for the camp, Lorna!"

So that for any romantic notions she might have begun to entertain.

For the next two weeks she was completely immersed in her work. It was almost unbelievable how many people needed the agency's help—and how often a skillfully guided discussion cleared up minor problems.

"You're a good counselor," Ellen told her one day. "It's not always easy to remember *not* to give these people advice. That, more than likely would make each one more firmly convinced that he or she was right. The trick is to make them think and arrive at the right decision, seemingly under their own power. You do it very well."

Lorna smiled gratefully, but after Ellen left, she sighed. There were times when she didn't do so well. For example, what had she done wrong with Ann who hadn't returned?

But Ann did, the very next day. Lorna quickly reshuffled some of her appointments so that she could fit the unhappy girl in.

Ann drooped. Her honey blonde hair was neatly combed, but her eyes were deeply shadowed. When she sank into a chair, her hands dropped limply into her lap. "My folks won't help me," she said dully. "They say I'll have to give the baby away. My mother is furious—and my father won't speak to me." Her eyes filled with tears. "Please help me, Miss Evans. If only I could find Chet, I know things would be all right. I love Chet. I know he loves me."

"Did your folks offer to help you find him?" Lorna asked gently.

"No. They said if he wanted to marry me, he wouldn't have run away."

"And what do you think?" Lorna persisted. This was the hardest line to take, but it was a kind of dreaming Ann was doing, building a fantasy because she did not want to face the ugly reality of the situation.

The girl looked at Lorna wildly for a moment, then her face dropped into her hands. "No, I suppose he wouldn't." She looked up finally. "But if I could talk with him . . . if only I could just once talk with him . . . I know everything would be all right!"

"Are you sure, Ann?" Lorna prodded gently. "He knows where you are, doesn't he? He knows you are pregnant?"

"But I know he loves me! We planned to be married."

Lorna allowed her to relate this, the most common story of girls in trouble. There were always the promises, the avowals of love, and too often when the girl had given herself, the promises faded away . . . and like Ann, the girl was left to face the guilt, the shame, the recriminations of her family—alone.

Ann stopped and Lorna said, "Do you think he plans to marry you now? Do you think he would run away if he had?"

The girl began to cry. "What can I do?"

"Perhaps the first thing is to face the situation realistically. I know that's hard, but until you face it, we can't plan what is best to do."

"I want to keep the baby. No matter what my folks say, I'll keep it!" Ann cried.

"Have you thought how you will provide for it?"

"I'll get a job. I'll earn the money."

"That's very commendable. And, if you have thought it through carefully, then I will help you plan for the baby's care," Lorna told her. "But I wonder—*have* you thought it through completely? Who will take care of the baby while you work? It will be very expensive to hire someone. Can you earn that much?" Lorna picked up a pencil, and item by item, helped Ann figure the cost of the baby's care.

"But that's more than I can make!" Ann exclaimed when she saw the total.

"I'm afraid so. Perhaps your mother would help?"

"No. I know she wouldn't." Ann's head dropped again into her hands. "I don't really blame her. My mother is proud. It would be terribly humiliating for her."

"Have you thought how distressing it may be for your child as it grows older?" Lorna asked.

"I'm sure my baby wouldn't grow up without a name. I'm sure once the baby comes, Chet will come around. He'd—"

"Do you think that by keeping the baby you will bring Chet to you?"

"Yes," Ann admitted. "I guess that's what I'm thinking. And why not? It will be his baby. How could he turn his back on his own baby?"

"It's hard to understand, Ann. I know. But hasn't he already turned his back? It's been more than two months since you've heard from him."

Ann hung her head. "I guess you're right. My mother said I should go to a maternity home."

"There's not much use of that if you plan to keep the baby, because people will know what's happened," Lorna reminded her. "But if you plan to give it for adoption, a maternity home is advisable."

"I don't know . . . Oh Miss Evans, I'm so confused."

"Would you like more time to think it out? We could wait another week or so . . . perhaps your mother may even change her mind."

"I do need more time," Ann said wearily. "I can't bear the thought of giving my baby away . . . and yet it does seem selfish to keep it, for the baby's sake, I mean."

"Whatever you do, the decision must be yours. Don't make it hastily."

The girl got up slowly. "May I call you if I need to?"

"Of course. Any time. If I'm not in, or if I'm having a conference, leave your number and I'll call back as soon as possible."

She watched Ann leave, sending a silent prayer with her. If only girls knew what lay ahead of them when they gave themselves to men. This was the third girl this month, in Lorna's own case load. Each one had been left to face her trouble alone.

Ann returned with her decision a week later. She was pale,

but more calm. "I've made up my mind, Miss Evans," she said quietly. "I'm going to give my baby for adoption."

"Very well, Ann." Lorna did not show her relief at the girl's decision. It would have been wrong for Ann to keep the child in her situation, and unfair to the child. There were so many families longing for babies to adopt, families who would give the baby a good home, love, every opportunity to grow up as a normal child should. She hoped she had not unduly influenced Ann, but only helped her to view the situation from every angle. "You're sure this decision is final?" she asked gently. "You won't change your mind?"

"I won't change my mind. I know I can't do what I want. I must do what is best for the baby." She bit her lip to keep it from trembling. "I know that Chet couldn't really have loved me. He never intends to see me again."

Within the shelter of her desk, Lorna clasped her hands tightly. It was so difficult in these cases not to go overboard with sympathy. Girls like Ann were so young . . . so vulnerable . . . and so hurt. If only . . . but in Ann's case it was too late for second thoughts. "Then you're ready to make your plans?" she said quietly, steering the girl toward the conclusion of this unhappy business.

"Yes. I want to go to a maternity home. I hope—could it be in another state, Miss Evans?"

Lorna had already talked with Grace Heaton about the possibility of a maternity home, so that she would be ready in the event that Ann decided to give the baby up. Now she nodded. "Yes, Ann. We can arrange to have you admitted to a home in another state. We'll make the plans at once."

For the first time a touch of color appeared in Ann's face. "Oh Miss Evans, I do thank you. My folks will help me with the expenses."

Lorna was pleased to hear this. It promised a better relationship for the girl later. But she said only, "That's fine, Ann, if they can. If not, we can arrange it."

"I'm glad I came to you," Ann said. "I know about girls who have gone to the wrong places for help and gotten into worse trouble. I heard about one girl who died—" She got up, leaning a moment on the desk, her face breaking with emotion. "I wish I could tell every girl in the world how phony a boy's promises are when he wants her to go all the way!" Her hands made small fists against the desk. "It's all so wonderful . . . till you're in trouble. Then you find out how much love there is in his lies. Oh Miss Evans, how can girls be such fools?" She made no effort to hide her emotion. "We ruin our chance for real happiness, we break our parents' hearts, we go through life making our children pay for our mistakes —or give the baby away—" She choked on a sob. "Now all my life I'll never know where my baby is . . ." Turning abruptly she ran from the room.

Lorna took a step to follow her, but heard the outer door slam and knew that she could not catch her. She found herself trembling. Most girls who found themselves in trouble were not as articulate as Ann, but they all endured the same shame, the same suffering. . . Lorna sighed and straightened her shoulders. She could not dwell on this, or on Ann's problem any longer. Someone else in trouble was waiting to see her. . .

She was limp by closing time. This had been one of the most difficult days since she had come to Family Service, and she could hardly wait to get home, get into a warm tub and then to bed.

As she stepped out of the building, she saw Marianne Blakely hurrying toward her. Something in Marianne's manner made her suspect that this was no chance meeting—and Marianne was the last person she cared to see at this moment.

Chapter Fourteen

"Oh, Lorna!" Marianne exclaimed. "I haven't seen you for ages! Not since you and Farley—" She broke off, as if embarrassed, but her next remark made it plain that the slip had been intentional. "You'll be glad to know that Farley has been consoled. He's engaged to Milli." She studied Lorna with cool blue eyes. "Greg and I are going to their announcement party at Milli's tonight."

Lorna said something appropriate, she hoped, but the unexpected news had shaken her—and she knew that Marianne had not missed the reaction. Only—it wasn't Farley's engagement to Milli that distressed her. After seeing those two the last time at the Tower, this announcement was a foregone conclusion. The sense of loss that she felt at this moment was on another account entirely and as she left the sharp-eyed Marianne, she hoped the latter did not suspect what that might be.

What a thoroughly depressing day, she thought, as she climbed into her little Volkswagen. At home she found a note from Nola saying that she had gone out with Peter, and sighed with relief. Nola was the best roommate in all the world, but tonight she did not want to talk to her—or to anyone else.

The bath revived Lorna sufficiently to make her hungry. She heated some soup and sat down to eat. As she did so she glanced at the clock and realized that the guests would be arriving at Milli's party just about now . . . Farley and Milli . . . Marianne and Greg . . . Suddenly she pushed the soup plate away and, covering her face with her hands, began to cry. She couldn't remember having cried like this in all her life. Her sobs had slackened to hiccupy sniffs when the jangling of the telephone sounded sharply in the room. She picked it up automatically and was startled to hear Greg's voice. "But . . . I thought you were at Milli's party!" she gasped.

"You knew about the party then?" He seemed taken aback.

"I ran into Marianne today and she—"

"I'd like to come up to see you, if it's all right," he said, breaking in.

"But the party—"

"I stopped by. I didn't stay for dinner."

"But Marianne—"

"What about her?"

"You're supposed to take her to the party. I mean, she said—" Lorna was sure she heard his deep chuckle. "Will you stop talking about non-essentials and let me know if I can come up to see you?"

"Yes, of course," she said, her hand fluttering to her hair. Had her bath made it too limp? Could she—

"Half an hour," Greg said.

"Yes . . . yes."

Hanging up the phone, Lorna raced into the bedroom to dress. Her hair was damp, but curled closely about her face. The reddened eyes would need treatment . . . She heard the doorbell as she was adding a touch of color on the lips . . .

Greg glanced at her searchingly then held his car keys up.

"I thought you might like to go for a ride. It's a wonderful night."

"Yes, I'd love to," she said, and hoped he had seen no tell-tale evidence of her earlier tears. In a little while she was quite sure that he had and that he had jumped to the wrong conclusion. How could she tell him she had not been weeping over Farley!

He drove south and it seemed no time at all until they reached the mountain highway where massive trees met in great arches overhead.

"My father's business is lumber," Greg said. "I grew up in the woods." He talked of his family, lovingly with deep respect.

Lorna found herself telling him of her people, of their struggles, in a way she had never talked to Farley. As they drove through the night she became keenly aware of his nearness. He continued to talk easily, on a variety of subjects —as if trying to distract her thoughts, she finally concluded. Had Greg decided that she needed comfort this evening and then volunteered the treatment? It would be just like him. She smiled ruefully into the darkness. Greg's big, kind heart included everybody—even girls with broken engagements whose ex-fiancés had just been "consoled."

Even so, when they returned, she felt calm and refreshed. There was a light in the apartment so she knew that Nola was home.

"Come up for a cup of coffee?" she invited.

When she started to insert her key in the lock, the door was flung open by Peter. "Come in, Lorna, my angel! Nola and I are celebrating." He offered his hand to Greg. "Congratulate me, old man. I've just let myself get roped into a wedding."

Nola appeared, looking radiant. "Roped in!" she cried. "Why, I didn't even have to ask him!"

"When?" Lorna wanted to know, kissing her roommate.

"Not until fall," Nola replied.

"I don't think I'll mind being married," Peter said, rotating a bottle of champagne gently in an ice bucket.

The bottle was opened with great ceremony and Peter poured it into goblets.

"To your happiness," Greg said, lifting his goblet. His glance touched Nola and Peter affectionately, and then rested on Lorna as they drank. She wished she could read his thoughts. On the other hand, it might be better if he could read hers, she decided.

The month of April passed swiftly. Lorna was so caught up in Nola's happiness that the publicity connected with Farley's and Milli's wedding left her untouched. Not even a twinge, she thought one night as she came across a picture in her newspaper showing the newlyweds setting off on a European honeymoon. Nola's happiness was contagious. She and Peter were so right for each other. As right as she and Farley were wrong, she thought wryly. She and Greg were included in the gay round of parties in honor of the couple, and although Greg went along willingly enough, she thought that he was rather quiet, as if often absorbed in more serious thoughts of his own. Greg was not a party-goer, any more than she was.

Lorna caught herself up short. She was devoting a great deal of thought to that young man. He was good company, but more than that, she felt the deeper meaning of his life and ambitions. Her feeling for him had grown without her being aware of it. It was not at all like the one she'd had for Farley—a flood of emotion that swept down upon her and would have swept her with it, regardless of any responsibilities she found important. With Greg it wasn't like that. His ideas and ideals paralleled her own . . . but he was still only a dear friend and associate, with whom she had frequent lunches and dinners at which they discussed cases and procedures and camp plans. Greg's work, also, was of paramount importance to him.

At the office Lorna was developing real skill in handling people—who were often much older than herself. She told Greg about one of the most touching cases during lunch one day.

"Two elderly sisters, Greg, one blind, the other a frail patrician lady of eighty-two. The blind one called the office while her sister was out. I wish you could have heard her sweet voice. 'Can you help us without my sister knowing?' she asked. 'She is going without food so that I can have it. She thinks I don't know because I'm blind.' "

Greg put his fork down and regarded Lorna steadily. "What did you do?"

"I got out there as fast as I could," Lorna said. "They lived in an old, old house—once very grand but now falling apart. I did my best to explain who I was without revealing the fact that the blind sister had asked me to come. The patrician sister stared at me icily. 'We don't need charity. We've always gotten along, and we'll keep on doing so!' I think she would have slammed the door in my face, but just then the blind sister spoke up. 'I called them, Jennifer. And we do need help. You've been giving me food and going without yourself. I wasn't sure until you fainted this morning.'

"Well, it took considerable persuasion to make Miss Jennifer see that she would become ill and unable to care for her blind sister if she persisted in starving herself. Finally she unbent and invited me to have tea with them, which she served in a most gracious manner. Then, with great dignity she consented to accept our help . . . Oh, Greg, if I had a million dollars—"

178 ·

"What would you do?" he asked, his nice gray eyes twinkling.

Lorna laughed. "I wouldn't have it for long, that's sure." She returned to the elderly ladies who had become her special pets. "The Public Assistance program is helping the sisters financially now, but I still visit them. It seems to give them such a lift—and I come away feeling as if some of their elegant manners had rubbed off on me."

"Now that is hardly necessary," Greg protested. "Your manners are perfect."

"Oh—you know what I mean," Lorna said, her cheeks pink.

"How about your other pets?" Greg asked. "I know you follow up every case."

"As much as I can, anyway." Lorna sighed. There were so many she couldn't follow up personally. "Judy's doing fine; and Glennie is a real pleasure. See?" She took out a typewritten letter from her purse and showed it to him, then read a few lines.

. . . This is a sample of my typing. I'm not very fast, but I am accurate, Miss Evans . . . and I can hardly wait for the day when I'll be seeing you in Tacoma. . . .

"I'm so proud of Glennie. I can hardly wait until she gets here myself." She recollected herself suddenly. "Oh dear, here I've been rattling on about my people without giving you a chance to say a word. How's the camp progressing?"

"Fine. We're just about ready to go. As you know, Nola has arranged her vacation so she can come out, and Peter has promised to come on weekends. Several social workers have been most cooperative, and I've arranged to have someone from the city's nursing staff to be on duty."

"And the children?" Lorna asked softly.

"I've screened them very carefully. It's essential to have the youngsters ready for such an experience. We don't want it to be a setback for any of them. I think I have a good, hand-picked group."

After lunch, he left her at the door of her building, and Lorna walked in with a light step. She always got a tremendous lift out of talking with Greg and now she swung into her office with confidence. She was learning to trust her own judgment more and more, and Grace Heaton had been very complimentary about her work. But there was still much to learn. The camp for disturbed children would be another kind of valuable experience, and she was looking forward to it. But, to be absolutely honest, Lorna thought, she'd have to admit that she was looking forward to working with Greg . . . and June was a flip of the calendar away.

On a Saturday morning in June, Lorna drove out to the camp with Nola. As they reached the crest of a hill and turned into the grounds, both girls exclaimed over its beauty. A large white house stood on a rise of ground, surrounded by low white cabins. The lake lay below, bright and shimmering, and the whole scene was framed by tall trees.

"What a peaceful place—what a perfect place for troubled young minds," Lorna said.

"I don't know how it could be any more perfect," Nola agreed.

Greg and two younger men named John and Gary came toward them as the girls drove up to the big house, but there was no time to talk as a busload of children arrived at that moment.

There would be fifty children, Greg had told them, and Lorna would be in charge of one of the smaller cabins with four of the younger boys whom he especially wanted to study. Norton Baxter, a Y.M.C.A. worker, and his wife, Jane, would be next door in a larger cabin. Nola would occupy a cabin some distance away, and younger counselors, like John and Gary, who were interested in social work, would be on hand to help out in various ways. Now Gary picked up the girls' luggage, so they could get settled in their cabins while the children were sorted out.

"In that way you can be ready and waiting for them," Gary said, flashing a nice smile which reminded Lorna of Greg. "Greg's instructions," the young man added. "That man thinks of everything." There was genuine admiration in his tone.

They reached the house and he carried her bags inside. "I'll go help with the kids now, if you don't need me," Gary said.

"Go right ahead. And thank you very much." She watched him lope out of sight, strong, vigorous, cleancut. Greg had a way of attracting nice people to his way of thinking, she reflected as she began to unpack.

She was in the cabin almost half an hour, unpacking, and checking over in her mind the various plans she had formulated after studying textbooks on disturbed children, before Greg came with her four boys. He had briefed her on their case histories before, and now, as he introduced them, she was able to identify each one.

Manny, the tow-headed youngster with the brown eyes, looked fiercely independent, his chin thrust out in a way that seemed out of character with his round face. Lorna wondered if the exaggerated fierceness were a shame to cover up his need for love. He was thin, and his disturbed state became evident in the activity of his hands, which scarcely ever remained still. Manny was nine. His home now was in the

State Mental Hospital with one hundred and twenty-five other disturbed children.

"Hello, Manny," Lorna greeted the boy warmly. "This will be your bed and dresser, right here. Want to start unpacking your things?"

Manny eyed her suspiciously, then nodded, and thumped his small suitcase on the bed.

Ted was eight, and functioning on the level of dull-normal intelligence, she remembered, although Greg had pronounced him average in mentality. He was from a home where he had been over-protected by his mother, but rejected by his father. Greg had said this child harbored deep feelings of insecurity and anxiety.

Lorna greeted him with a smile and indicated his place in the cabin, then turned to Boyd. Greg had said that his problem was lack of impulse control. As Lorna studied him, she couldn't recognize this; he seemed perfectly normal, red-headed and alert. She settled him and faced her fourth charge.

This was Jon, who was preoccupied with fantasies of aggression toward his older brother. Yet outwardly he appeared passive, his secret feelings hidden from her. He was ten, a thin lad with crewcut blonde hair. As soon as Lorna welcomed him, Greg left to attend to his many other duties.

The four boys stared at Lorna shyly, speculatively. Their vulnerable youth tugged at her heart and she hoped she would prove capable of dealing with them wisely. Perhaps a good way to get acquainted would be to take them on a tour of the grounds as soon as they were settled here.

She suggested it, and the boys set about their unpacking with a spurt of energy.

It was during the walk that she began to discern their individual problems and struggles, but they did seem to like her. At least they stayed close to her—or did they regard her as a marker in a strange new world? She studied each small head bobbing beside her and longed to clear it of the cobwebs that set its owner apart from normal children. She had only two weeks . . . but two weeks could mean a great deal in their young lives. Greg had said he would talk to her about these boys after she had met them . . .

She looked for him on the grounds when her little party returned to their cabin, but he was busy elsewhere. Anyway, he was *here* and so was she, and they were sharing a common interest.

"Come on, fellows," she said to the boys, "let's find out about dinner!" and the little troupe followed her obediently.

Chapter Fifteen

Lorna discovered that the children required constant vigilance. All their games and activities had to be carefully planned and supervised. This was her first experience with children so young and she felt a tremendous responsibility toward them. Wisdom-packed textbooks were one thing, but young minds flying at slightly warped tangents were something else. Of course Greg was there to advise and consult, but there were many details of the boys' daily life that she had to think out and direct by herself. Each child was an individual, and each one could go and should go only at his own pace. It was astonishing how quickly her four small charges crept into her heart.

Red-headed Boyd's problem came into the open after two days at camp. He began to reveal his disturbances by bullying the other boys. He was sly about it, and it was not always easy to catch him, nor to protect the younger boys from him, especially Jon.

One day, when she had taken the boys for a hike, Boyd broke away from the group and started climbing up a rocky crag, showing off before the others. Suddenly he froze there, near the top, and terrified, began to cry and call for his mother. The other boys began to shriek at him, and laugh and Lorna had a moment of horrid panic. Suppose Boyd fell! If only Greg were here! But Greg was out on the lake with a group of his own.

Taking a deep breath, she spoke calmly to the other children, then calling softly to Boyd, she started up the crag, finding foot and hand holds somehow. Within reach of the frightened boy, she stretched out her hand, palm up—and suddenly his small hand was in hers, his confidence returned. They made their way down without mishap—and from then on Boyd appeared to be more relaxed, his association with the other fellows more natural.

Jon puzzled Lorna at first, especially since Boyd had chosen him as the main target of his bullying. No matter how Boyd taunted him, Jon would not fight back but stand with his hands clenched. Lorna remembered something she had read in a case history. After rest period that day she gave Jon a pad and crayons and suggested that he draw whatever he liked. He sat staring at the blank pad for a while, then suddenly his crayons flew and the play-figure of his older brother emerged—as a victim for all sorts of destructive acts.

Then, later, when Boyd was teasing him, Jon came to Lorna and asked if he might fight back. She nodded, hiding her apprehension. But the fight that ensued was normal boy-business which cleared the air and after that there was no more trouble between Boyd and Jon.

Eight-year-old Ted, however, seemed to take little interest in anything. His thin shoulders hunched apprehensively as he sat and watched the others. Lorna put him in bathing trunks and set him up with finger paints. In no time at all Ted was absorbed in a fascinating new activity—all traces of which could be removed by dunking him in the lake. Before long he began to enter into group activities, tentatively, yes, but still, he was venturing out among his fellows on his own.

Watching her little brood in a game of ball, Lorna realized that she would miss these boys when the two weeks were over. Manny, most of all, for he seemed to have the greatest need of her attention. She knew she must not let him depend on her . . . but he so desperately needed love, and when she read to him, his restless hands would lie quiet, and he would crowd close to her shoulder. One day he said to her, "I don't want to go back to that place."

"You mean to the hospital?" she asked gently.

"It's a crazy house."

"It's a place where people are ill, Manny. You will be well one day, and then you can go home."

Manny lifted brown eyes to hers. "I don't want to go home. I want to come with you."

"You can't come with me because I live in a small apartment. There would be no place to play, and I'm gone all day. It wouldn't work, Manny."

"You don't like me," he declared.

"Of course I like you. I like you very much. And I will come to see you at the hospital."

"I'm not going back."

"When is your birthday, Manny? I'll come to see you on your birthday," Lorna promised.

He brightened a little, and she talked to him about his birthday, of what present he'd like her to bring him. The others joined them then, and Manny did not pursue the subject. He had not mentioned it since. Thinking it over later, Lorna was sure that Manny had only wanted to test her, and that he had forgotten the incident.

She was writing a report near the window of her cottage when she saw Nola and Gary come out to play ball with the

186 ·

children. Nola had entered into the spirit of the camp with real enthusiasm, and the children adored her. Happiness shone around her like a halo these days, especially when Peter came for the weekends.

For one sharp instant Lorna envied Nola. It must be wonderful to feel that certain of one's future. From the first Nola had never doubted that she loved Peter. Why couldn't love be as simple for her, Lorna wondered. How could she have thought she was in love with Farley? For him she had felt a keen attraction, a physical awareness, a fascination, and if they could have found a deeper bond, a common interest, the feeling might have grown into real love. Marriage had to be built on a much sounder foundation than she'd had with Farley. She saw Greg cross the lawn. Her feeling for Greg had come unbidden. She had not wanted to fall in love again so soon, yet in the past weeks this feeling had grown unmistakably.

Manny came running into the cottage. "Come play with us, Miss Evans!" he begged. She gave him her hand and allowed him to pull her out to join the game until time for the rest period before dinner.

She was returning to the cabin when Greg called to her. Waiting for him she noticed how sun-browned he was. In spite of his almost ceaseless duty, he looked vigorous and refreshed.

"I'm sending Gary over to your cabin to stay with the boys during the rest period," he told her as he came up. "I think you need a break. Would you like to hike up to the cathedral?"

Quick pleasure at the invitation flashed to her. The "cathedral" was a natural shrine of virgin timber, where immense trees formed a circle. Log benches had been put there, and many groups coming to the campsite used it as a place of worship. On Sunday they had taken the children there. It would be a lovely spot to be with Greg.

"The camp has been a wonderful success, Greg," she said as she fell in step with him. "It's a real victory for you, proving that a camp like this can be of real value."

He smiled his slow, gentle smile. "Some people were skeptical all right. You've done a great job, Lorna. I've been observing your work with the boys. You have a natural gift, you know."

She felt a warm flush in her cheeks. Greg was, himself, so dedicated, this was high praise, indeed.

They were entering the stillness of the tall trees now. Greg gave her his hand to help her over one of the big logs which edged the clearing. As she jumped down, he held her hand a moment longer than necessary, looking down on her. Suddenly, behind them, they heard a small voice.

"Miss Evans! Miss Evans!" Lorna turned toward the slope and saw Manny breathlessly running toward them.

Greg frowned. "The boy should be in his cabin, resting." This was the nearest to impatience she had ever seen Greg come. She felt impatient, too, disappointed that this moment had been stolen from her, but she said, "Let him come. He has run all the way here."

Manny confessed that he had climbed out of the cabin window, so Gary wouldn't see him. Now he clung to her hand, nor did he release it until they were returning down the slope, when he ran ahead.

"This is our last night here," Greg said, looking around regretfully. "Would you like to go out in the boat tonight after the camp has settled down?"

"I'd love it," she told him.

188 •

It was nine-thirty before the children appeared quiet for the night. Lorna left Jane Baxter with the boys in the cabin and found Greg waiting for her at the lake's edge.

The lake was beautiful. As they glided away from the shore in one of the small boats, the moon cast a silvery path for them on the water. Lorna watched Greg rowing rhythmically, saw him reach for his pipe without losing a stroke. He did not speak, but his gaze returned to her again and again. The water lapped at the boat. There was magic about the night . . . the solitude, the beauty . . . as if it wrapped them in an infinite timelessness. Lorna wondered if Greg felt it, too, but she did not trust herself to speak. Stretching out her hand, she let the cool water wash over it.

Greg leaned toward her, the oars resting . . .

Then sharply out of the silence came a long-drawn "Hallo-o-o-o—"

Greg raised his head, listening. The call came again. "That sounds like Gary. He's calling me." Quickly, capably he turned the boat around. "Something's happened. Gary doesn't excite easily." He rowed back swiftly. Gary was standing on the shore, Norton Baxter beside him, others crowding around.

"Manny's disappeared," Norton told them as they pulled into shore. Gary stepped into the water to help beach the boat.

"Manny!' Lorna gasped. "But I left him in bed. I was sure he was sound asleep."

"Jane doesn't know when he sneaked out," Norton said, "he was there when she checked after you left, but when she went in a few minutes ago, he was gone." He turned to Greg. "I've already formed a search party. Chances are he's made off into the woods—" Lorna noticed then that the people were in groups. "I figured one group could go off to the big timber and one to the cut over land on the west—"

Lorna was thinking frantically. Manny had said he "wasn't going back"—but—"Wait!" she cried. "I don't think Manny would go into the woods. He's terrified of the dark." She had given him a little flashlight to keep when she had found him sitting bolt upright in bed at two o'clock in the morning.

Greg turned to her. "I think you're right—"

"I shouldn't have left him," Lorna lamented.

"Don't be silly." Nola's arm slipped through her own.

"Jane's at the cabin having hysterics," Norton said worriedly. "She wouldn't come out for fear one of the other boys might take off."

"Go up to her, will you, Nola?" Lorna asked. "I can't leave here until we find Manny."

Nola gave her arm a firm squeeze. "Don't get yourself into a stew, sweetie. He'll be found."

"Now, where would a boy go who is afraid of the dark?" Greg was obviously thinking aloud. "He wouldn't go to the woods; he wouldn't go upshore—he'd stay close to the buildings—" He paused, thinking it out carefully. "He wouldn't hide near his own cabin because that would be the first place we'd search, and he wouldn't crawl under a house because that is unknown and darker than the outdoors. But he might hide under—"

"A boat!" Lorna and he shouted it at the same time.

Greg was already hurrying to the place where four boats lay bottom up on the sandy beach. Lorna was right behind him.

"Manny," she called softly. "If you are under the boat, please come out."

There was a moment of silence. Then faintly a scratching could be heard and a small voice. "Miss Evans, Miss Evans."

Lorna ran to the boat and Greg lifted it. There was Manny, fully dressed, wide-eyed and frightened. In one hand he clasped a small bundle and the flashlight which was not turned on. In the other he held a rock. He raised the rock above his head. "I'm not going back. I told you I wasn't going back, Miss Evans."

"Oh Manny," Lorna said. Ignoring the rock, she stepped forward, took the bundle from him and clasped his cold hand in her own. "Come, Manny. Let's go back to the cabin."

Slowly Manny put the rock down and the three of them walked up the slope. At the steps of the cabin, Greg turned to Lorna. "I think Manny and I have something to talk over. Do you mind, Lorna?"

She shook her head. But when Greg led Manny away she didn't want to go into the cabin. Manny's escapade had really shaken her. She wanted to absorb the peace and serenity of the scene about her—and to think. Slowly she moved toward the beach and stood there, gazing out over the lake, listening to the night sounds.

She did not hear his footsteps because of the gentle lapping of the water. Then Greg's voice said, "Manny will be all right. I think we got a few things straightened out in our talk . . ."

"You didn't scold him, did you?"

"No. I merely pointed out how we all have to do certain things which we must do. He seemed to understand."

"Poor little fellow," Lorna said, feeling her cheeks grow wet.

Suddenly Greg's arms were about her. He reached up and pressed her head down to his shoulder. "Poor Lorna. You want to give so much to so many. Would it help if there were —two of us, working for the same things?"

She had relaxed against the comfort of his shoulder, but now she looked up into his face, startled.

"Is it too soon after Farley?" Greg asked gently.

"Oh, Greg!" She clung to him, burying her head. "It never could have been Farley," she told him, her muffled words coming through to him. "He never understood—anything. That's why I broke the engagement."

"You did?" He held her off for a moment, then his arms tightened so that she could scarcely breathe. "You did!" There was a world of relief in the exclamation. "Oh, Lorna, and here I've been waiting—I think I've loved you from the first moment I saw you." He lifted her face and kissed her.

"You'll name the date—soon?" he whispered.

"Yes—oh, yes. Very soon," she promised. There was no need to wonder, to consider, to weigh this or that with Greg. With Greg she *knew*.